THE GHOUL OF CHRISTMAS PAST

STEVE HIGGS

BOOKS

Vinci Books

vinci-books.com

Published by Vinci Books Ltd in 2025

1

Copyright © Steve Higgs 2020

The author has asserted their moral right to be identified as the author of this work in accordance with the Copyright, Designs and Patents Act 1988. This work is a work of fiction. Names, characters, places and incidents are the product of the author's imagination or are used fictitiously. Any resemblance to actual persons, living or dead, places and incidents is entirely coincidental.

All rights reserved. No part of this publication may be copied, reproduced, distributed, stored in any retrieval system, or transmitted in any form or by any means, including photocopying, recording, or other electronic or mechanical methods, nor used as a source for any form of machine learning including AI datasets, without the prior written permission of the publisher.

The publisher and the author have made every effort to obtain permissions for any third party material used in this book and to comply with copyright law. Any queries in this respect should be brought to the attention of the publisher and any omissions will be corrected in future editions.

A CIP catalogue record for this book is available from the British Library.

Paperback ISBN: 9781036708665

The EU GPSR authorised representative is Logos Europe, 9 rue Nicolas Poussion, 17000 La Rochelle, France contact@logoseurope.eu

By Steve Higgs

Blue Moon Investigations

Paranormal Nonsense
The Phantom of Barker Mill
Amanda Harper Paranormal Detective
The Klowns of Kent
Dead Pirates of Cawsand
In the Doodoo with Voodoo
The Witches of East Malling
Crop Circles, Cows and Crazy Aliens
Whispers in the Rigging
Paws of the Yeti
Under a Blue Moon
Night Work
Lord Hale's Monster
Herne Bay Howlers
Undead Incorporated
The Ghoul of Christmas Past
The Sandman
Jailhouse Golem
Sparks in the Darkness
Shadow in the Mine
Ghost Writer
Monsters Everywhere

Modern Fairy Tale
No Such Thing as Magic

Albert Smith Culinary Capers

Pork Pie Pandemonium
Bakewell Tart Bludgeoning
Stilton Slaughter
Bedfordshire Clanger Calamity
Death of a Yorkshire Pudding
Cumberland Sausage Shocker
Arbroath Smokie Slaying
Dundee Cake Deception
Lancashire Hotpot Peril
Blackpool Rock Bloodshed
Kent Coast Oyster Obliteration
Eton Mess Massacre
Cornish Pasty Conspiracy
The Gastrothief
Lyme Regis Layover
Majestic Mystery

The Ghoul

SATURDAY, DECEMBER 24TH 0615HRS

The sense that he was being watched crept over him as he left his house in the predawn gloom. Jason Pendergrass was one of those lucky people who was born into money. He'd never worked, not really. His great-grandfather made the family fortune with an engineering firm he started. In the beginning, it made buttons, of all things, but at the advent of the Second World War, he secured funding to convert the factory to produce bullets and later components for armoured vehicles.

Selling over-priced parts that could not be obtained elsewhere proved to be highly lucrative, most especially when Jason's own father spotted the trend toward computerised components and plugged a whole pile of money into R&D. Now they led the market in thermal imagery and targeting equipment and he couldn't spend all he had coming in even if he tried.

His father forced him to learn the business and take a job on the board, but ironically, it bored him. Less than a week after his father's untimely death, Jason stepped down and focussed on doing things that were fun instead.

He was up early this morning to pursue one of his favourite hedonistic activities: snowboarding. He was taking three girls to Tignes in France where he planned to bed all of them. One at a time, or all together, he really didn't mind. That they were each at least twenty years younger than he didn't bother him either. They were old enough to know how the game was played, so he was paying for the trip and they would foot the bill in a different manner.

He couldn't help smiling to himself as he pictured it.

That was until the little hairs on the back of his neck began to stand up. He was still living in his parents' three-million-pound Georgian house in Higham. Sure, one could argue that he still lived with his mother at forty-seven, but she wouldn't last much longer so soon the house would be his and he could avoid paying inheritance tax because it was his house too.

The Range Rover was part loaded, but the rest of his gear was still in the house, necessitating several more trips back and forth. He cursed himself for being too lazy to pack yesterday. Had he done so, the handyman or the gardener could have been employed to help him load the car. At this time of the day, there was no one else around.

He paused at the rear of the car, squinting into the darkness. Was there someone there? A chill breeze ruffled his hair, what little of it he had left, and he bit his lip in indecision. He opened his mouth to call out, 'Is there someone there?' but realised how clichéd that would sound and so stopped himself.

With a harrumph, he went back to the house, berating himself for being scared of shadows like a child.

Fifty feet away, a shadow detached itself from the pocket

of dark in the lee of a tall tree. The shadow was over seven feet tall and appeared taller yet because it wore a top hat, the very top of which was torn so it stuck up at a raked angle. The tall shadowy figure lumbered across the lawn heading for the car but approaching from the front and away from the lights projecting outward from the building.

Moments later the lights came on anyway, the motion sensor triggered by Jason as he struggled out with all the remaining bags, boots, and boards in one load. Something in the dark was creeping him out, so he was going to throw the remaining items on the backseat of the car and get going. The girls were expecting him to collect them soon anyway. He wanted to be on the slopes by early afternoon, and on one of the girls by early evening.

Unable to shift the creepy feeling, he threw his armful through the backdoor as fast as he could and slammed it shut. He didn't care that it was a mess that would most likely tumble out as soon as he opened the door again. He would sort it out after he collected Sophie or, rather, when he collected her as he would need to load her items then.

Without a care that the sudden noise of the rear door slamming would most likely wake his mother, he jumped into the driver's seat and slammed that door too. The engine was already running, chugging away to make the car's interior warm and power his heated seat. Now that he felt much more secure, he stomped on the gas and peeled off down the drive with a slew of gravel.

Fifty feet away, back at the trees, a figure leaned out to watch. No longer concerned he would be spotted and give the game away, the figure, far more normal sized than the first one, started walking after the car. He didn't hurry his pace though: the car wasn't going to get very far.

A snort of laughter escaped Jason's nose as he settled in

and wondered what on Earth had got into him. Jumping at shadows at his age? Ridiculous.

The house's long driveway bent around in a big arc to reach the front gate which would automatically open once he got close enough to it. Relaxing, he turned his attention to the stereo. He needed to portray the hip, edgy personality that would lure the girls into his bed. No good listening to Radio Two which was universally considered to be for old people even though he always listened to it when he was alone. As his finger poised over the button to select Crushing Crew Beats volume two, the sensation of being watched returned but in a far more serious way.

Checking his rear-view mirror to see if he were being followed, he found it to be filled with the ghoulish head and face of a giant man. The apparition's pallid skin had the anaemic appearance of a corpse and when he opened his mouth, the sound that came from it was a bone-chilling rasping noise that defied translation.

Jason Pendergrass screamed in fright, an automatic reaction he could not have fought and failed to even try.

Giant hands surged forward, grasping his head on either side as the ghoul came between the front seats to get him.

Across the garden and watching with excitement as he strolled nonchalantly after the Range Rover, the second smaller shadow saw the car swerve and look ready to lose control. For a moment, he worried it might leave the driveway and crash into one of the ornamental displays, of which there were many dotted along the route in and out of the grand house. That wouldn't do at all, so he was thankful to see the car come to a stop to the side of the driveway but still on it.

The victim was in for a real treat, even if he didn't know it yet.

Breakfast

SATURDAY, DECEMBER 24TH 0900HRS

'There is something screwy here.'

Mary Michaels raised an eyebrow and looked up from her newspaper. She did not agree with conversation over breakfast, she felt it interrupted the flow of her day. Raising her newspaper so it formed a shield in front of her face, she focussed on the article she was reading.

Two fingers looped over the top edge of the newspaper to pull it down. On the other side, her husband, Michael Michaels grinned a cheeky grin at her.

'Good morning, Mary,' he said as if they had not already spoken several times in getting up and starting their day. 'I wonder if perhaps you were too absorbed in what you are reading to have heard me speak?'

'I heard you,' she replied, casting her eyes back to the page.

Michael waited to see if she had anything else to say, and when it became clear she did not, he persisted. 'I believe I have stumbled across something.'

Mary felt that she had to deal with enough nonsense

from her son, Tempest's, shenanigans already. With a sigh, she made eye contact. 'Have you finished your breakfast, dear?'

Michael cocked an eyebrow and looked down at the wreckage of his two boiled eggs with toasted soldiers. 'Yes, dear.'

'Then perhaps you ought to stumble across the kitchen where you will be able to put away the condiments and wash up the dirty plates.' With a flick of her hands, the newspaper once again formed a barrier between them.

Frowning at the Prime Minister's face as it leered out from the front cover of his wife's broadsheet, Michael Michaels tossed a mental coin. Should he push the issue and risk an hour or more of sullen silence as his punishment or withdraw his hypothetical troops from her border? 'There was a theft from the Dickens Museum a few days ago,' he chose to go with full invasion.

With a huff, because she liked to make her feelings abundantly clear, Mary Michaels folded her newspaper, placed it neatly on the table, and fixed her husband with a glare. 'What of it? You told me about it when it happened.'

'Yes, dear, how silly of me to trouble you with conversation.' Her glare intensified. 'You may remember my old Navy buddy, Rob Whittaker. Well, he was talking about the theft the other night in the veteran's bar.'

Mary frowned. 'I do not recall him talking about that.'

'You didn't hear him because you were chatting with the ladies. He said he was the one who reported the theft and that it was mighty strange because the items had been there on his previous pass. When he came back the next time, they were gone, but all the doors and windows were locked. He suggested it was an inside job and had said as much to the police. He'd been called to see the curator of the museum the following day.' He did some mental math. 'That would have been yesterday then. He was expecting a commendation of some kind for his diligence and for handling the situation without feeling the need to phone management et cetera. He also expected they wanted to quiz him about the other guards because if it were an inside job, they might consider him to be the only one they could be sure to trust.'

'Why?'

Michael gave his wife a surprised expression. 'Because he's the one who reported it. If he were also the thief, he'd be a terrible one.'

She nodded, not particularly interested. 'Why are you telling me this?'

Glad she asked the question, Michael got to go back to the original point. 'I mention it now because I note while reading the news myself, that one of the shareholders for the Dickens Museum has gone missing.'

'Missing?' Mary echoed. Then sensing that she had foolishly shown interest, begged, 'So what, Michael? Why are you telling me this?'

'Because that's two things … two crimes in the space of a few days at the same place. Doesn't that feel like it must be connected somehow?' He watched her face for sign that she saw the connection too. When she showed none, he asked, 'Don't you think these things might be connected?'

'A missing person is not a crime,' she replied, lifting her paper once more and opting to be pedantic because it annoyed him when she did. 'Not until a body or a ransom note turns up.'

Michael sniffed in a breath through his nose, breathing deeply and holding it for a second while he squinted his eyes in thought. 'No. There is something screwy about this.'

Now she got it. 'Oh, no.'

'Oh, no?' he repeated her words. 'What oh, no?'

'You're trying to be a detective,' she accused him. 'I knew this would happen. The moment you started getting involved in Tempest's cases, I knew it would come to no good. And I was right, wasn't I?'

Trying not to frown across the breakfast table, Michael nevertheless felt that his wife might be missing the point. 'A man who owns shares in the Dickens Museum has gone missing and things have been stolen from the Dickens Museum.' He remembered something else, adding quickly, 'And let's not forget that Dickens Greatest Works Theme Park just shut with the loss of all jobs. There must be a connection in these things. It stinks like a cover up or a diversion tactic.'

'That's your son talking. That's the exact sort of thing he would say and since he is the private investigator and you are just a retired Royal Navy officer, perhaps you should let him know about it and leave it at that. Besides, the Dickens Museum and Dickens Greatest Works Theme Park are completely different entities, I don't even think they are owned by the same people.'

Michael skewed his lips to one side. 'I don't know. You might be right,' he conceded.

'There you are then,' said his wife, collecting her newspaper again and considering the subject closed.

Generally opting to take the path of least resistance with his wife – it had ensured for a happy marriage thus far - Michael pushed back his chair and began to pick up the crockery and cutlery. 'What's that website Tempest uses to find out about people and companies and stuff?' he asked, taking an armful to the kitchen.

Mary elected to not answer his question, choosing to

divert his attention instead. 'We have a few jobs to do today,' she announced. 'I'll need your hand with the groceries, there are books to return to the library, and there's your prescription to collect ...'

His wife's voice faded into the background as he concentrated. There would always be mundane things to do like shopping for lettuce and taking books back to the library. Those tasks could be performed any old time. In the morning, they were driving to Hampshire to spend Christmas with their daughter and her husband and the grandchildren. That was exciting and he looked forward to it. His children and more recently his grandchildren were a blessing. He had to wonder how long it might now take Tempest to produce a child, given how enamoured he appeared to be with his business partner and girlfriend, Amanda.

Thoughts of his children and grandchildren were all very nice but seeing his grandchildren didn't get his pulse racing the same way running around with Tempest did. It wasn't that he was bored exactly, he wasn't looking for an adrenalin rush, at least not consciously. However, the years were creeping on, and a milestone birthday was just around the corner. If he didn't do the things he felt like doing now, soon he might decide he was too old to do them. There might be nothing to the Dickens events, but equally, they could be connected, and it sounded like exactly the sort of thing his son, Tempest, might choose to look into.

'Companies House!' he barked triumphantly when the name suddenly popped into his head. Now all he had to do was work out how to look up the information he wanted.

A face appeared around the doorframe, pinning him to the spot with squinty eyes and a narrow expression.

In his head, Michael Michaels prayed she wouldn't raise

her wagging finger. She reserved it for those rare occasions when she wanted to really give him a telling off and he didn't feel it was currently warranted. Granted, he was giving serious consideration to doing just exactly as he felt and had been known to get himself in bother when the mood took him, but the wagging finger only ever led to arguments between them and he didn't want that right before Christmas.

She placed her hands on her hips, which gave her husband reason to make a relieved noise. 'You don't have time to be getting distracted with any nonsense today, Michael,' she warned. 'We are going away in the morning so you need to pack, and we have jobs to do as I have just told you, and, in case you have forgotten, which you probably have, we are going to the theatre this evening.'

'How could I forget that?' he asked, posing a question because then he hadn't actually lied. She'd only been talking about it yesterday, but it had completely slipped his mind again. This was probably due to the fact that he didn't want to go. With Dickens being such a local influence, stage productions of his works were held regularly at different venues. Each Christmas, an open-air performance occurred in the castle grounds which forms a natural bowl. He could agree that the setting was dramatic and impressive, but he would rather volunteer for a rectal exam from a man with hooks for hands while simultaneously retaking his year ten algebra exam than spend three hours trying to stay awake through another Dickens production.

He had no one to blame but himself of course. This year's tickets, much the same as last year's and the year before that were due to foolishly lying about how much he enjoyed it the first time she took him. Had he been truthful and revealed that he would rather spend the evening singing

Barry Manilow songs naked at an outdoor piano bar in Siberia, then he would have suffered swiftly but not perpetually.

Mary left him with the dishes as was their custom and went to find her coat, shoes, and handbag. There seemed no escape, but taking out the trash, he sneakily checked over his shoulder and made a phone call.

Captive

SATURDAY, DECEMBER 24TH 0942HRS

'Are you comfortable?'

The question was posed by a person wearing a fancy Victorian frock coat in a very dark green. Beneath it, a black waistcoat that matched the trousers complimented the outfit which was then completed by a top hat and a shiny black swagger stick with a silver ball on the top. He also wore a mask which many would instantly recognise to be that of Charles Dickens. Quite why he appeared in such a strange outfit was not known by the man on the floor to whom the question had been posed.

Charles Dickens – we might as well call him that for, unable to see his face, we have no idea as to his true identity – knew he would not get much of an answer because the man on the floor was gagged as well as bound. Dickens wanted to land a few well-placed kicks to the man whose eyes were bugging out of his skull in terror now. It wasn't just this one he wanted to punish, of course, there were four of them in total and each carried the same level of irresponsibility and greed.

Struggling against his bindings, Jason Pendergrass was clearly trying to say something, making unintelligible noises while trying to gesticulate using only his eyes.

Sighing, Dickens picked at the duct tape until he worked a corner free, then ripped it off in one vicious, yet satisfying motion. 'Yes?'

'Who are you?!' That Jason Pendergrass chose to blurt those three words almost cost him his life. If Dickens had a weapon to hand, he would most likely have used it, but since he didn't, he chose to stop resisting his natural desires and kicked his captive straight in the ribs.

The burst of air from his victim's lungs pleased the man in the Charles Dickens mask but disappointed him at the same time. 'You see? That's the real problem here, isn't it? How can it be that you don't know who I am? You ruined everything for me. Stomped all over my work which I spent the last two years putting together just so that you could get even richer than you already are, and you don't even recognise my voice. I think that about says it all.'

Jason couldn't believe this was happening. He was the victim of a madman and being beaten mercilessly though he had no idea why. And where was that horror who grabbed him in his car? Jason never wanted to see him again as long as he lived. No sooner had the thought presented itself than the oversized ghoul lurched into view.

Though his back was already against a wall, Jason nevertheless tried to back away, wriggling his shoulders and hips to squirm across the floor. 'Waaaaahh!' he gibbered, showing off his Eton education.

Charles Dickens snorted. 'Are you afraid of my ghoul? Good. So you should be. One word from me and he will rip your arms from their sockets.'

The ghoul showed no sign of moving to do so. Nor did

he smile at the mental image, but it was small comfort to Jason, who was just about ready to wet himself. 'Why am I here?' he begged to know. 'What do you want from me?'

The man in the mask pursed his lips – not that his victim could see it - and thought about how to answer that question. 'I want from you the same thing I have always wanted: your support. If you would just stay out of the way and stop making stupid decisions, I would make you rich.' Jason couldn't help his confused expression forming. What on Earth was the mad man jabbering on about? Seeing questions forming on his captive's brow, Charles Dickens started to back away: now was not the time to explain. 'This will all make sense soon, Mr Pendergrass, I promise. Now, if you will excuse me, all is not yet ready for the presentation and I must get back to work.'

The ghoul lingered, unsure what was expected of him since no instruction had been given. When he glanced down at the man on the floor, he saw the fear in his eyes. The ghoul blinked twice and tried to communicate a question.

On the floor, backed hard against the cold, damp wall, Jason was horrified by the noise the creature made. It appeared to be trying to say something, but the sound was nothing but a low wailing moan, a mournful noise that spoke of terrible things to come.

When it grabbed Jason in the car, he'd lost control instantly and shortly thereafter lost consciousness. Jason didn't know where he was, but when he came to, he found his bindings were far too tight to move around or escape from which made his location a moot point. The three girls he was due to collect were bound to report him missing at some point, but until then, no one would be looking for him – he was supposed to be on his way to France to spend Christmas on the slopes.

The Ghoul of Christmas Past

The monster reached an enormous hand down to Jason's face, causing his squirming motions to return. 'Get away from me,' Jason squealed, fear making his bladder threaten to betray his commands.

The ghoul's hand stopped moving forward, pausing for a moment before withdrawing. Jason stopped squirming; he had nowhere to go anyway. Mercifully, the horrific apparition stood up once more, showing off his full height, and left him where he was. Walking away, Jason got his first good look at the beast. It had to be over seven feet tall and looked to have been hewn from a girder. His arms, legs, and shoulders were huge blocks of meat and his chest was a barrel holding it all together.

The ghoul rounded a corner and was lost to sight, giving Jason some hope that he might be left alone and could work on trying to escape. However, when a door clanged shut with a resounding thump, the creeping sensation that he was locked in as well as tied up stole over him. Would it matter if he couldn't break free of the bindings? Why was he here? Why him? The mad man made it sound like he had a specific reason for kidnapping him, but for the life of him, Jason had no idea what it was.

The Library

SATURDAY, DECEMBER 24TH 1119HRS

The shopping took longer than it needed to in Michael's opinion. It was as if Mary had chosen to deliberately drag her feet and peruse the goods in each aisle with far greater scrutiny than ever before. Was she doing it just to make sure he wouldn't have time to get up to anything else?

Michael Michaels kept his lips sealed on the subject, knowing there would be no benefit to starting a fight about it. Instead, he used the time to ponder what he thought to be a case worthy of investigation and tried to phone Tempest again.

His phone showed six calls had now gone unanswered and this one was no different. Whatever Tempest was doing, it was demanding his undivided attention. Given that Michael's son had only gotten out of hospital the previous afternoon after a close run with hypothermia, he didn't find it too surprising that he couldn't get an answer – it did worry him a little though.

Was he okay? Sure, Tempest was as tough as they come, his military training had seen to that, but he was still human. Staring at his phone, which he hadn't had long and was still getting used to, he grumbled, 'I'd send you a message, son, if I could work out which button to press.' Pocketing it again, Michael told himself the most likely cause for his son not answering the phone was that he was sleeping late to regain the lost hours the previous case stole. It was that or he had Amanda with him and could hear the phone but sure as heck wasn't going to answer it.

'What are you doing, Michael?' Mary's voice invaded his thoughts, grabbing his attention just as he guiltily realised he hadn't been listening to her.

'Yes, dear?'

'The gravy granules.' It was clear from her tone it was not the first time she had asked.

'These ones?' he groped for a familiar looking brand which drew a sound of impatient disgust. He tried again.

'Oh, goodness, Michael,' Mary sighed as she stepped into his personal space to pluck the ones she wanted from the shelf by his hand. Thinking it would have been simpler for her to have done that in the first place, he maintained his policy of keeping his mouth shut. 'You're away with the fairies today,' she muttered, tossing the box into the shopping trolley. 'Whatever is it you've got in your head?'

She was daring him to bring up the subject of the Dickens Museum again, and he wasn't falling for that trick. Hitting her with an engaging smile, he said, 'Nothing, dear, I was just basking in the warmth of your love and drifting along on the enchanting scent of your perfume.'

Had her eyes gone any narrower when she cut them at him, she wouldn't have been able to see. 'You are up to something, Michael Michaels, and I don't like it.'

'I'm sure I have no idea what you mean, dear.'

The rest of the shopping proceeded as planned, at least

so far as Mary was concerned, but her husband was acting decidedly odd.

From the supermarket, they parked outside the library and walked across the road to the pharmacy opposite. Mary much preferred using the local shops because she knew the owners and was able to have a chat with them. There were so few left though. When the children were still children, she had been able to get everything she wanted without needing a car and without travelling more than a mile in total. Now, only a handful of the shops were left.

At the library, Michael left Mary to check in her books, and made an excuse to abandon her, 'Call of nature, love. I shall not be long.'

He was already moving away when she turned her head to say, 'I'll wait in the car. Don't be long, we bought frozen things.'

The library was due to close in just a few minutes but perhaps that was all he would need. The entrance to the research library was right next to the toilets which he genuinely needed to visit. Michael didn't lie to his wife, it was yet another policy for a good marriage so far as he was concerned, but he had to be convenient with the truth sometimes, or choose when to reveal the bigger picture, as it were.

Hurrying along the short corridor to the research room, he spotted a librarian and went directly to her. Keeping his voice low in deference to his location, even though there were no other patrons present that he could see, he asked, 'Can you assist me with a tiny bit of research?'

The lady stared at the clock, drawing Michael's eyes there too. 'We close in eight minutes.' It was a response but not an answer in Michael's opinion.

Having no intention of being put off, he started toward

the bank of computers set out around a rectangular table in the middle of the room, calling over his shoulder, 'Good thing this will only take four minutes then.'

The lady followed him with a disgruntled sigh, so full of Christmas spirit it was spilling over. 'What is it you need help with?' she asked wearily.

Maintaining his own chipper attitude, Michael replied, 'I need to look something up on Companies House. You know, where they register all the businesses and list the directors and such.' He was sitting in the driver's seat in front of the computer, and ready to go. Or would have been but for one small barrier: he didn't even know how to turn the computer on.

The woman cocked an eyebrow. 'I'm not sure what it is you need help with. That is just a simple search. You do know the name of the company you wish to look at, yes?'

Admitting the truth, Michael jumped out of the chair again so the lady could replace him. 'Yes, I want to see who the directors of the Dickens Museum are, but I don't know how to perform a simple search as you call it. I wouldn't even know where to start.'

The lady blew out a breath of frustration, checked the clock again, and climbed into the chair where she tapped the mouse to bring it to life. Seconds later, she leaned to one side so Michael could see the screen. Just as he requested, the lady had brought up the pages for the Dickens Greatest Works theme park on Companies House. He'd never looked at this website before so could not tell what he was looking at or if it was as it ought to be.

Nevertheless, there was information. 'Can you print that?' he asked, 'I guess you want to get away so that might be the swiftest way to get rid of me.' He tried a warm smile, found it bounced off her grim stare like snow melting on a hot roof, and asked, 'Any chance I can get pictures of the people named?'

Two minutes later, shocked at how fast the printer operated, Michael Michaels left the library with a quick pace as staff gathered by the door waiting to lock them.

The carpark was almost, but not quite devoid of cars, though he suspected all the cars that were not his were those of the staff now heading for home and their families. He bade everyone a, 'Merry Christmas,' crossing the car park and waving to the 'helpful' staff as they replied in kind. Spotting the stern-faced lady blithely ignoring him as she hurried away, he tried to quickly devise a cool line to offer her. None came, and had it done so he would have only her back to talk to as she never even looked his way.

However, Mary did, and she had a look that suggested she was displeased to see a ream of paper in his hand. 'What is that?' she asked as he slid into the passenger seat.

He hadn't had a chance to look at it properly, and hadn't seen any of the pictures yet, but quickly shuffled the pages to find them now and his eyes jutted clean out of his head. 'That's him!' he blurted.

'Him who?' Mary could see that Michael was trying to show her a picture, but she was driving and unwilling to look.

Staring at the page, he told her, 'The man in the bank last week.'

Mary was getting annoyed with her husband's unexplained comments. 'What man?'

Michael answered his wife, 'The one who was shouting,' but his thoughts were already on something else as he tried to remember what the man had been shouting about. It had been something to do with destroying jobs or ruining livelihoods. He strained his brain, demanding it recall the man's ranting with a little detail.

'What man?' Mary repeated, not used to being ignored.

'The one in the bank,' Michael attempted to explain. Perhaps Mary would remember more than him. She'd commented on his need to use profanity as he stormed from the meeting room he'd been in. 'Don't you remember? He slammed the doors and swore at the manager.'

They stopped at some lights, allowing him to hold the picture up again. 'Oh, him,' Mary took a glance and recognised the man instantly though he was smiling in this picture and very much hadn't been when she last saw him. 'He was most upset about not getting a loan for his business, wasn't he?'

Her statement jogged Michael's memory. 'Yes, that's right. He said they lacked vision, just like everyone else and they would all see the truth soon enough. He is listed as a shareholder ...' Staring down at the page, his jaw dropped open. 'That's the man that went missing earlier this week,' he blurted.

Mary asked, 'Who is?'

She got the page waved in her face in response. 'The same guy. The same guy we saw in the bank shouting at the manager last week is the one who was kidnapped.'

'You don't know he was kidnapped,' Mary argued.

Michael didn't bother to argue, mostly because his wife was right, but also because he was reading down the page. 'It says he has a hundred shares in the firm. It's the same people running the museum and the theme park.'

Mary reminded him, 'No one is running the theme park now. It closed.'

A hundred shares. Was that a lot? Michael knew little of such things, but it didn't sound like a lot. He flicked to the next page, finding Mason Sabre and then Jason Pendergrass, discovering that both men had several hundred shares each. Checking more pages, he found there were a total of five shareholders, and four had a sizeable portion of the firm in their grasp. Ronald Norton, the missing man who needed a loan, had only a fraction. Michael skewed his lips to one side as he thought about it, but concluded, 'These things must all be connected.'

Engaging her sweet voice, the one which said he better dare not take another step, she said, 'I thought we agreed you wouldn't be looking into any of this silly Dickens' stuff. We don't have time, and that's your son's job not yours.'

'But ...'

'And he wouldn't investigate it unless he had a client,' she added when he tried to speak.

'But what about ...'

'And you would only embarrass yourself and get arrested if you were to poke your nose where it isn't wanted. You're not as young as you used to be, Michael.' She managed to make her last comment sound loving.

'Hold on a second.'

'So that's it settled then,' she concluded. 'Jolly good. Let's get home and pack and then we can have a nice cup of tea. It will be time to get ready for the show soon.'

Michael waited for her to finish, and once he was sure she no longer expected a response from him, he launched his salvo. 'I may not be young, dear, but my brain works perfectly well and there is something happening that no one is dealing with. I need to visit Frank. If there is something going on, he'll know about it. Tempest often says he goes to him to get the inside scoop on the weird things around here.'

Mary screwed up her face. 'Frank? That horrible little man in the comic book shop?'

'Yes, Mary. I'll tell you what. If Frank says there is nothing happening at the Dickens Museum or that there's nothing odd about the theft or the missing shareholder,' he rifled through the pages again to find the one who was missing. 'This fella, Ronald Norton, then I'll drop it all and won't mention it again.'

Mary cut her eyes across the car, sensing a trap. 'And if he says there is something screwy? I've met him, Michael. I have the impression that he thinks everything is screwy. Didn't you tell me he was in that Kent League of Demonologists?'

'If he says there is a pack of vampires behind it all, then I'll call Tempest and I'm sure he'll be glad of the case. He can take it on because, you know, I'm so decrepit.' He mimed gumming with no teeth and being hunched and geriatric.

Wondering if it might be the only way to shut him up, she sighed. 'Fine. But if the three-bird roast I just bought for New Year's defrosts while you are mucking about, there's going to be trouble.'

The Dickens Museum

SATURDAY, DECEMBER 24TH 1202HRS

They chose to park behind Tempest's office where they expected there to be several empty parking spaces. They were not disappointed. The office was locked as they expected it to be, and when they made their way through the pedestrian gap in the wall to reach Rochester High Street, they found the office lights off.

Mary asked, 'Why do you seem surprised that no one is working? Why would they be?'

'I don't,' Michael replied, frowning at the office's dark interior. 'Tempest isn't answering his phone, and that usually means he's off doing something.'

'He only got out of hospital yesterday,' Mary pointed out. Michael raised an eyebrow, his expression clear. 'Okay,' she conceded with a sigh, 'I suppose that wouldn't make much difference where Tempest is concerned.'

'No.' Michael crooked his arm and offered it to his wife. She slipped her hand into his elbow and let him steer her. However, her feet stopped the moment he started moving.

'You're going the wrong way, aren't you?' she questioned. 'I thought the place we want is on North Gate?' She referenced the road not the ancient structure which both bore the same name.

'I thought we might stop for a Christmas Eve sherry,' he announced, tugging her along. For good measure he bent his head to nibble at her neck playfully.

Mary swatted him away. 'Get off me, you old pirate. We're in public for heaven's sake. Behave.' The sherry sounded good though, and a nice change of pace to running from one task to the next which is how Christmas always seemed to be. 'Where shall we go? It's been so long since we stopped for a drink on the High Street.'

Her observation saddened Michael a little but he made a mental promise to make up for it when he turned her to the left. 'Oh, look, dear. The Dickens Museum is open. I think we should pop in. I've been curious about this place for ages and never once thought to visit even though it is right on our doorstep.' He was laying it on extra thick. 'So much history around us, but we blunder through it barely noticing ...'

He became aware of a spot of heat on his left ear and turned his head to find Mary boring a hole in the side of his head with her eyes. 'I'm going for a sherry, Michael,' she hissed. 'So you stop all the nonsense about history and go do your silly investigation thing. I'll get you a sherry too, but if you are not quick about it, you may find nothing but an empty glass when you return.' Then she pulled her arm from his and flounced into the nearest public house.

Michael puffed out his lips, almost went after her to apologise but knew well enough that no good would come of it. She would just continue to guilt trip him into doing things her way if he gave in so easily. The museum wasn't going to be open for much longer – everywhere was closing early for Christmas. In fact, checking his watch he had little more than twenty minutes, and that was going to have to be enough.

At the ticket booth, he got a surprised look from the chap behind the glass. 'We close in a few minutes,' the man said. He looked to be in his eighties, though still full of life and energy. So much so that Michael hoped he looked half as good in a few years' time. The man didn't have a lot of hair left but what there was, the man, who had a name plate labelling him as *George*, had left to grow long and styled it over his head from front to back.

Michael held out a twenty. 'I just need to see a couple of things. You can keep the change if you can give me directions to find them quickly.'

The man stared down at the note for a second or so, licked his lips nervously and then pulled down the blind on his booth. Thinking he might have somehow insulted the old man and missed his chance to see the museum at all, Michael was about to put the twenty pound note away when a side door opened and the man came out.

'For twenty, I'll show you myself,' George said gleefully. Leading Michael through the museum, which was poorly lit for effect, he said it had been years since anyone gave him a tip and even longer since the company gave him a bonus. He made it sound like getting the change from a twenty had made his year. As they went, Michael pulled off his gloves, hat, and scarf. He was too hot in them now he was inside and would feel all the better for being able to put them on when he went back out.

'What is it you want to see, sir?'

'Michael, please,' Michael insisted. He'd never liked being called sir even when he wore a uniform and it was a requirement of the rank. 'There were some items stolen from here a few days ago. I was hoping you might show me where they were taken from and tell me what they were.'

If the question surprised George, he showed no sign, amiably chattering away with a plethora of Dickens facts as he led them through a series of passageways.

'Here we are, just up here on the right.' They stopped in front of a display which had a curtain erected in front of it. A free-standing sign on a steel pole declared the exhibition to be under repair. George moved the curtain to one side so Michael could see, but there was, of course, nothing to see at all because it had been stolen.

Studying the empty cabinet, Michael asked, 'What was in here?'

'One of Mr Dickens finest outfits. It was a long green coat with real silver buttons. Ever so fancy it was. It had a walking cane with it as well, plus a top hat.'

'Did it have any value?' Michael asked, curious as to why anyone would want to steal it.

George sucked on his teeth. 'I couldn't rightly say. I mean, I'm sure to the right collector it would be priceless.'

Michael nodded. 'But otherwise, apart from its historic value, it is essentially worthless. Why steal a set of Charles Dickens' clothes?'

'That was what Robert asked,' replied George. 'That's Robert Whittaker, I should say, the man who discovered the items were missing. He used to be a guard here,' he explained.

Michael had been about to reveal that he knew the man in question when he caught what the old man had said. 'Used to work here? As in past tense and he no longer does?'

George had wide open eyes as if he'd just been caught

selling state secrets. 'Why, yes. He was fired yesterday. Fired by Professor Loughborough, the museum's curator.'

The news came as a shock. Fired two days before Christmas when the man thought he was in for a commendation. 'What on Earth was he fired for?' asked Michael, then seeing George's face, he paused to explain, 'Sorry, I should tell you that Robert and I are old friends from the Navy. I spoke to him just a couple of nights ago and he thought he was getting a reward for discovering the theft.'

'Oh, goodness, no,' gasped George, now looking about nervously to see if someone might be within earshot. 'Robert told the police it had to be an inside job. Told them he checked every way into or out of the museum when he discovered the theft, and that there was no sign that anyone had been in. He even checked the cameras and they had been switched off. Professor Loughborough was furious with him. We could all hear the shouting. It wasn't like we wanted to but noise travels in this place.'

'What did the professor say, exactly?'

'That he agreed with Robert and it had to be an inside job but that since no one came or went and he was the only guard on duty that night, it had to be him that stole it.'

Michael screwed up his face. 'But that doesn't make any sense.'

George gave a half shrug. 'I guess Professor Loughborough figured that the best way to cover up the theft was to pretend to be the one to discover it.'

Michael could see a bunch of holes in that theory big enough to drive a truck through, but he didn't bother to continue questioning the man from the ticket booth. It was now past closing time and George probably had a wife waiting somewhere who would be pleased to see him.

Michael did too for that matter, though he was fairly certain his sherry glass would be empty.

He turned back the way they had come. 'Thank you, George. You've been most helpful and have given me plenty to think about.'

'I have?' George sounded like he didn't know what that might be.

Michael nodded anyway. 'Perhaps we should both head back to the doors, so I can leave, and you can finish for the day.'

Making their way back the way they came and going slow, for George was not a speedy walker, Michael poked his nose at some of the other displays they passed. He'd been singularly focused on the way in, paying little attention to any of it, but now he stopped to take it in. Behind glass panels, and carefully lit with dim watt bulbs, were pages handwritten by the great man himself. His diaries were also on display, so too items such as pipes and favoured items of clothing. First editions of his books which had to be worth an absolute fortune. Michael paused by one display.

'How often are these cabinets cleaned?' he wanted to know.

George blinked. 'Cleaned? I couldn't say. They look like normal cabinets, but I know they are not. They ...'

'They are part of a very expensive controlled humidity environment,' said a voice from out of the blue. It came from ahead of them, though Michael did not see who had spoken for another half second. A tall, thin man with round glasses came toward them out of the dim passageway, continuing to speak as he did, 'One advantage of that, is they very rarely require cleaning because the air is filtered in and carries next to no dust.' He was in his fifties, Michael judged, and had an air about him that suggested he was an athlete of some kind, a cyclist maybe. The man kept coming, stretching out his hand to greet Michael. 'Professor Loughborough. I'm the curator here.'

Michael took the man's hand, squeezing it tightly. 'Michael Michaels.'

The professor turned toward the nearest cabinet, one containing several books. 'The air inside the cabinets has to be kept at a carefully managed temperature and moisture level to maintain the books, and many other artefacts, in the best possible condition. They have enormous historic significance – Dickens was arguably the best author ever to walk the Earth, but even those who might argue would accept that he is among the greats and was most certainly the greatest of his era.'

Michael offered no argument.

The professor turned his attention to the man from the ticket booth. 'George, what are you doing back here? You should have finished and gone home already. Edith will be waiting for you.'

'Yes, Professor,' George replied with a dip of his head. 'I was just showing this gentleman to the exit.'

The museum curator placed a friendly hand on the old man's shoulder. 'That's okay, George, I have it from here. A merry Christmas to you and yours. I'll see you in a few days.'

'Yes, sir. Merry Christmas to you too.'

George hurried away, but Michael Michaels stayed where he was, staring into the cabinet. Before the professor could speak again, Michael went to look in another.

'Is there something amiss, Mr Michaels?' the professor wanted to know.

Michael didn't answer straight away because he was

trying to work out if he was right or not, and if he was, what that then might mean.

'Mr Michaels,' the professor prompted him, his voice now containing a slight air of impatience.

Michael judged that the man was getting close to advising that the museum was officially shut and to ask him to leave so he surprised him with a question of his own. 'Why did you fire Robert Whittaker?'

The museum curator was caught off guard, but only momentarily. 'Who are you?' he demanded to know.

Michael pressed on, walking toward the professor with purposeful strides. 'That is not an answer,' he pointed out.

The professor looked like he was about to argue but caught himself before he started. A small smile crept onto his face. 'Shall I call the police? Or will you leave peacefully, Mr Michaels? The museum is closed, and you have no further business here.'

Michael Michaels stared up at the taller man for a few seconds, thinking through his options. 'I'm deciding,' he told the curator when it looked like he was going to ask the question again.

'Is everything all right, Professor?' This time the voice was that of a security guard who Michael judged was probably performing a routine walkthrough simply because he knew his boss was in the building. Once the professor left it would be TV on, shoes off, and feet up.

Only a blind man would fail to see the tension between Michael and the professor, so the guard came to stand beside his boss, both now looking at Michael Michaels.

'Still deciding?' asked Professor Loughborough with a small smile.

Michael came a step closer to him, demonstrating that he wasn't intimidated by the guard's presence. Never once even looking the guard's way, Michael said, 'Someone has been in the cabinets and I think you know about it.' Making such a bold statement gave away that he had seen the small marks on the shelves where the books had been recently moved, but it also meant he got to see what the curator's eyes would do when he accused him.

They widened in shocked panic. Like an eyeball gasp, it was uncontrollable and unmistakable.

Michael stepped back again. 'Thought so.' The professor was guilty of something. The question was not only what was it, but how could he be caught? Tempest might have the answers. Deciding he was done with the museum, Michael started toward the exit, going around the two men to get there. Over his shoulder, he called, 'Merry Christmas, Gentlemen.'

No one came after him or tried to stop him leaving, which was a relief because Michael had no idea what he had just been witness to. There was something going on, but he only knew that because he could see the facts failed to align and the professor acted guilty when he challenged him. Walking to the door, he made himself go slowly but felt like running because the curator could be a serial killer and trying to cover his tracks for all Michael knew.

What Michael didn't see, once he was outside and moving away, was the curator slipping out behind him. The tall thin man was instantly cold because he'd left his coat behind – there wasn't time to fetch it from his office, this was far too urgent. He ran to his car, going away from Michael Michaels, and holding his phone to his ear as he went.

The second his call connected he started talking. 'Someone knows.'

Anyone listening would then have heard a pause while he listened to the person at the other end.

'I don't know. Some older gentleman called Michael Michaels.'

A pause.

'No, he's not police.'

A pause.

'What do you mean, don't panic? I'm telling you they know. This is your fault. You're going to have to give it all back. I need to cover this up before someone else comes snooping. Maybe next time it will be the police.'

A pause during which Professor Loughborough plipped his car open and got in, transferring the phone from one hand to the other while he listened to the annoyingly calm voice at the other end.

'Listen, I'm coming to you. You can threaten me with blackmail all you want. I know you are up to something too. You give me back the things I let you have, and we'll call it even.'

The professor stabbed the button to end the call without waiting for a response and put his car in gear. He was a damned fool for being greedy in the first place, but he was a clever man, and he could figure a way out of his current situation. If that idiot Whittaker hadn't overreacted and called the police, there wouldn't be a problem now, but all was not lost.

He just needed to act fast and take control.

Preparing

SATURDAY, DECEMBER 24TH 1250HRS

'Is everything in place?'

The two men hearing the question could not tell which it was aimed at, and neither wanted to answer because the man asking it did not deal well with bad news. Everything was very much not yet in place. That had been a deliberate strategy on their part, but one which was now making them both feel very nervous. They looked at each other, both telling the other with their eyes to get on and speak.

When no answer returned in the two seconds following his question, their boss turned around to look at them. The men were dressed much like construction workers everywhere in hardwearing clothes streaked and stained with grime and fluids that would never wash out. They both wore bright yellow vests and hard hats though there was no one employed here to insist they follow health and safety guidelines.

They were not incompetent, far from it. The man scrutinising them hired them himself specifically for their skills, but they acted as though they were afraid to deliver bad news. It made him angry or would have if he allowed anger to ever cloud his judgement.

They knew him as Mr Dickens though neither believed it was his real name. What he called himself wasn't important because he was paying them double what they usually got, and they were between contracts anyway. The job had to be finished today, just in time for Christmas, so all things considered, they had been over the moon when the opportunity landed in their laps a week ago.

The men were new hires, taken on specifically to perform one important role and both were well-trained in their field. They were keen and pulling out all the stops because he had promised them a fat Christmas bonus if they got the work done.

'You have news which you do not wish to deliver?' the boss guessed, narrowing his eyes at the man on the left.

Now on the spot, Blake felt pressured to answer. 'We are nearly ready,' he lied.

The man calling himself Mr Dickens had the kind of education that would scare most academics and his skills as a business leader had been honed by years running different firms as he scaled the corporate ladder. He was a man going places, a man with a grand plan. However, his plan recently ran into an unexpected hitch and he was really rather angry about it. Angry enough to kill, one might say.

'Tell me,' the boss demanded, 'in very precise terms, what is yet to be done.'

Blake gulped; there was no way to avoid telling him the truth now. 'The job really needs more than just the two of us. We are nearly there but rigging all that explosive …'

'Yes?' Dickens prompted.

Blake licked his lips; this was their opportunity to cash in big time. 'Well, this sort of thing needs permits.' He let the statement hang in the air. 'Usually.'

Blake's partner, Edward, felt his colleague was making a mess of it, so jumped in himself. 'We're the ones taking all the risk here, Mr Dickens. If the authorities were to find out we didn't have the correct permits in place ...'

Like Blake he left the obvious part of his statement unspoken. They could both tell the man who hired them understood what they were saying.

Which he did. Mr Dickens sniffed and nodded. 'How much?'

'It's not so much about the money,' Blake tried to defend his honour and then had to stifle his squeal when Edward kicked his shin because it was all about the money and nothing else. They had spent the last two nights discussing how much they could squeeze this guy for.

'How much?' Mr Dickens repeated, impatience in his tone.

Edward swallowed hard. They had agreed on a figure of two thousand last night. Less than that wouldn't be worth it, and more would probably not get paid.

'Five thousand,' Edward blurted, making Blake's eyes bug out in shock.

The man narrowed his eyes and fixed them both with a look that might have turned them to stone in ancient Greece. 'Fine. But I want it done by five o'clock. Not a minute later. Am I understood?'

'Perfectly, yes, Mr Dickens,' they both responded instantly, unable to believe their luck.

'I'll have to go to the bank. I'll have your money for you before you finish.'

Blake and Edward hurried away, eager to get the job finished now. They would have it done before five o'clock if it killed them. This was the best Christmas bonus ever. They had no idea what the crazy guy had planned but they were in an old, abandoned theme park so whatever he planned to blow up wasn't going to hurt anyone and could never be traced back to them.

Mr Dickens watched them go and sat back onto the corner of his desk. 'Fools,' he growled. 'Greedy, grasping fools.' He wasn't going to the bank, of course, he had other tasks to perform. Jason Pendergrass, languishing in his makeshift dungeon in the basement needed to be joined by others yet. Edward and Blake, two former military engineers were necessary for the job, but were never going to survive to be paid. They were loose ends and soon to be taken care of by the ghoul. The ghoul, the man calling himself Mr Dickens smiled - what a lucky find he had been.

Mystery Men Bookshop

SATURDAY, DECEMBER 24TH 1331HRS

It was still crisp and cold outside, so upon exiting the museum, Michael zipped up his coat again. It was only a short walk to the pub where he found Mary sitting in one corner knitting. Two empty sherry glasses sat on the table beside a third one which was still full. Seeing her husband approach, she gave a smile and picked the sherry glass up.

When he got near, she held it up for him and as he reached for it, she pulled it back and drank it in one hit.

Michael knew he deserved it and raised his hands in surrender. 'Do I take it you have had enough now and would like to go, or shall I get us two more so we can actually spend some time together? Honestly, I had no idea it was going to take that long in the museum.'

Mary could see that he was being genuine, so patted the chair next to her and didn't kick it over when he went to sit in it, though the idea did occur to her. A barman brought them two more drinks, and they spent half an hour chatting about the grandchildren and reminiscing about Christmases when Tempest and Rachael were young.

It was a welcome break for them both, but to Michael's surprise, it was Mary who chose to move them on. 'If you want to visit Frank's bookshop, you'll have to get going. That three-bird-roast really will defrost if we leave it much longer.'

Michael suspected it wasn't in much danger of defrosting at all since it couldn't be more than about two degrees centigrade outside, but he kept that to himself. Once again, they walked arm in arm along the ancient cobbles, this time toward North Gate and the castle where they would be returning in a few hours. The High Street was filled with people doing late Christmas shopping – panic shopping might be a better word for it, Michael thought. Of course, there were people just out enjoying the ambience and visiting the many bars and restaurants the area boasted.

As they walked, Mary dialled her son's phone. It connected instantly.

'Mum, what's up?' Tempest's voice rang in her ear.

'Hello, Tempest. Your father claims that you are not answering your phone. Clearly, he was mistaken or phoning the wrong number perhaps. His brain is getting a little patchy.'

Michael, hearing his wife mention their son's name, swung his head her way and heard what she said. His frown amused Mary.

Tempest replied, 'No, I have a bunch of missed calls from him. I just haven't had a chance to call him back. It's kind of a busy day.'

'Why, what are you doing?' she wanted to know. Michael was leading her to the right, away from North Gate to place it behind them. The entrance to the bookshop was right in front of them, and Michael paused to let Mary's conversation finish. He also made it obvious he wanted to talk to his son before she hung up.

She could hear Tempest sucking on his lip, a habit he'd formed as a child which generally meant he was going to lie about something. 'Um, it's a bit complicated to explain,' he replied. 'I was planning to not work for the next few days, but something came up. Do you know what dad called for?'

'Something came up?' Mary repeated. 'You mean you're working a case?' she demanded to know. 'It's Christmas, Tempest. You ought to be spending it with family.'

'You are heading to Hampshire, Mother, and we agreed I would spend the time with Amanda and see you in a couple of days.'

'Not if you are working a case, you won't see her,' she argued.

'Amanda is with me, Mother, and this case really will not wait. Is dad there?'

Disgruntled, she thrust the phone at her husband. 'He wants to talk to you.'

'Tempest,' said Michael by way of greeting once he had the phone to his ear.

'Hey, Dad. Listen, don't tell mum, but Jane went and got herself kidnapped.'

'Jane?'

'Yes, Dad, Jane, the one I just asked you not to mention to mum. Amanda and I are tracking the person who we think has her, but there is … well, let's just say I am worried and don't have time to talk, okay?'

'Sure thing, son. I won't take up your time. Go do what you need to do.' The Michaels men rarely said it, but they both had deep-rooted love for each other. Father and son were cut from the same cloth and got on as well as two men could. More than that, though, Michael was impressed by his son and continually proud of the man he had become.

'What did you call for anyway?' Tempest asked before his father could hang up.

'Oh, err. I'm not sure I should trouble you with it now.' Mary rolled her eyes. 'It's about the Dickens Museum.'

'Is this about the ghoul?' Tempest queried.

Michael's right eyebrow raised without being told to do so. 'A ghoul?'

'Apparently so. I haven't been engaged to investigate it, but there were a bunch of sightings right before the Dickens Greatest Works Theme Park shut its doors a month ago. I know that's not the same place, but I figured the two have a lot in common. Why are you asking?'

Michael wiggled his nose. Why was he asking? 'I spotted something in the paper, a run of coincidences you might say. One of the shareholders went missing a couple of days ago, some things were stolen from the Dickens Museum, and the shareholder who went missing, well, your mum and I saw him in the bank last week and he was yelling blue murder about not getting a loan he needed. Also, I just met the museum curator and I'd bet my left nut he's hiding something.'

Tempest really didn't have time to be thinking about another case. Everything indicated that the Sandman was going to kill Jane tonight unless they worked out who he was and where he would be and then stopped him. Nevertheless, it sounded like his dad was on to something. 'Dad, your best bet is to talk with Frank.' Tempest shot his cuff to check his watch. 'He'll still be working, I expect. Try calling him at the shop.'

'I'm standing outside it now.' Michael placed his hand

over the phone to tell Mary, 'Tempest says I should ask Frank. He also says there is a ghoul at the theme park.'

Mary gasped, then realised what she had done and rolled her eyes again. She wasn't going to let her husband and his daft need for adventure get any rope because once his brain got running with an idea, it was difficult to stop.

'Dad, I've got to go. I'll let you know when I get Jane back. Take care of mum and have a good time in Hampshire.'

Michael opened his mouth to reply but the line went dead. He'd got some information from the call, but more than that, he'd listened to the steel in his son's voice. Tempest's determination to succeed galvanised Michael's own efforts. Retirement might be alright for some, but he needed a little something more than a few hours a week at the Royal Navy Dockyard to keep his mind busy.

Mary took the phone back when he offered it but did not like the look of her husband's gait when he pushed the door to the shop open and started jogging up the stairs.

The Mystery Men bookshop was the brainchild of Frank Decaux, a little man with big ideas who had made a small fortune very quickly through some astute business decisions, a lot of hard work, and really, really knowing his subject matter. That the shop doubled as a front for arcane practitioners to get their information, artefacts, and weapons was kept quiet, though he wasn't actually doing anything illegal.

Frank believed in everything mysterious, supernatural, paranormal, or unexplained. It wasn't so much that he thought it was real, but that he fervently hoped it was. Since before his age reached double digits, he'd read about the exploits of monster hunters and beast masters, of vampire lords and werewolf clans and wanted to be part of that world. He also recognised that at a shade over five feet and four inches and weighing in at barely a hundred pounds, he wasn't going to do much damage swinging a blade. Instead, he resigned himself to being the purveyor of information and found a niche where he was of great use to all manner of idiots who believed the same utter claptrap as he did.

His shop was on the second floor above a space that had been a dozen different businesses in the last few years. Currently it was owned by some ladies selling rubbish silver jewellery, but what went on below had no bearing on his business which thrived on the internet as much as it did anywhere else.

The jingle of the door drew Frank's eyes from the cash register as he looked across to smile warmly at yet more customers. He saw instantly that it was not, in fact, people coming to buy his wares, but Tempest's father coming through the door, followed a second later, by Tempest's mother.

'Brother Grey Fox,' Frank hallooed across the shop, drawing the attention of the mostly male crowd perusing his shelves. Tempest's father was a chap cut from the top drawer in Frank's opinion. If anything, Frank liked him better than Tempest who could be a bit prickly at times.

'Grey Fox?' repeated Mary, certain she had heard Frank correctly but unhappy about her husband having a nickname.

Feeling more in his comfort zone now he didn't just have his wife to contend with, Michael tipped her a cheeky wink. 'It's my biker gang name, babe.' Mary did not approve of him calling her babe, but he was a rogue if she didn't keep him on a tight leash and coming here was obviously the wrong thing to let him do.

Frank came out from behind the counter to shake

hands. 'Brother Grey Fox, what brings you to my establishment?'

Michael slapped his palm into Frank's and gripped his hand tightly. 'Brother Grizzley, I have a question for you, and I feel it is the type of question only a man armed with your knowledge might be able to answer.'

Unable to believe her ears, Mary interrupted. 'Brother Grizzley, Brother Grey Fox? Just what are you two raving lunatics on about?'

Taking a moment, Michael turned to his wife. 'Sweetums, it's man stuff.' Her hastily hitched eyebrow ought to have acted as a warning sign, but he barrelled on anyway. 'Frank and I were both inducted into a biker gang a while back while tackling a werewolf pack. You were at a Cliff Richard concert, sugar. It's nothing for you to worry yourself about.'

Not for the first time today, Mary narrowed her eyes at her husband. 'You are up to something, and I don't like it. Do you hear me, Mr Michaels? You are going to get yourself into trouble if you are not careful.' That she meant trouble with her and not some insignificant law enforcement agency or otherwise undisclosed third party did not need to be explained. Not waiting for a response, she moved away, feigning that a display of miniature figures from *Hell Boy* held her interest.

Frank watched her go, unsure what the interplay between man and wife had been about. Dismissing it, he got down to the business at hand. 'You said you had a question.'

Michael caught Frank's elbow and used it to steer him back to the counter. Behind it, two young Chinese women were serving a queue of customers with smiles in place. Michael didn't really notice them, not in the way that the other men in the shop did. Poison and her cousin, Athena, were around twenty years old and had that toned, athletic look that a person gets from spending a lot of time doing hard physical activity. In their case it was mostly martial arts that burned their calories and kept them lean, but they were both pretty to boot. Whether that was a happy coincidence or another example of Frank's astute business brain in operation could be debated.

'Frank what do you know about recent events at the Dickens Museum?' Michael wondered if it might be better to give Frank a little more to go on than the wide question he asked but phrasing it like that he wasn't leading him to talk about any specific topic.

Frank's eyes instantly flared, and he stepped closer so he could drop his voice to a whisper. 'You're talking about the ghoul, aren't you?'

Michael pursed his lips. 'Truthfully, I don't know. I only heard about the ghoul from Tempest a few minutes ago. I was referring more to the disappearance of one of the shareholders recently and a theft from the Dickens Museum. I thought the ghoul had only been seen at the theme park. Do you know different? I wondered if the events might be connected.' He produced his wad of printed pages from the library.

Frank looked at the pictures. 'Which of them has gone missing?' he asked.

Michael had to shuffle the pages again, awkward to do without a surface to spread them out on. Finding the right one, he placed the loose leaf on a handy bookshelf so they could see it. 'It's this guy, Ronald Norton. Mary and I saw him rowing with a bank manager last week when he couldn't get a loan. He went missing from his home three nights ago. His wife found a shoe and evidence of a struggle. The police are treating his disappearance as suspicious according to the paper.'

Frank sucked some air between his teeth and murmured, 'I worried this might happen.' Seeing his comment required some explanation, he said, 'With the League gone, the forces surrounding our mortal realm and attempting to push their way in have no one to resist them. The work the League performed in silence for centuries has suddenly been stopped and the barrier is removed. This ghoul has taken residence in the area and …'

Michael raised a hand to stop Frank. 'What is a ghoul? Layman's terms please.'

'Yes. Yes, of course. I always had this with Tempest too. One moment.' Frank held up an index finger to beg a moment's grace as he bent down to examine a nearby bottom shelf. Spotting what he wanted, he snagged a thin book and opened it. Michael leaned in to see what Frank wanted to show him. The bookshop owner leafed through a few pages to find the one he wanted. 'The term ghoul or, more accurately, ghul, originates in Syria. Described as a huge, humanoid beast and associated with graveyards and the undead, ghouls attack people and carry them away to eat them.'

Michael pulled a face. 'You think Ronald Norton might have been eaten?'

'If this is a ghoul, then yes, I guess it is possible. The descriptions, shaky though they are, are of a huge man with a deathly pallor. I think visitors to the theme park, and the press, thought it was a publicity stunt to draw more people in even though the park was failing, and the closure had already been announced. It made the headlines.'

'It did?' Michael had missed it completely.

'Well, not in the national tabloids, obviously. But in the

Supernatural Times it was a feature story.' Michael felt like rolling his eyes but held back. Frank was talking again anyway. 'You said there was a theft from the Dickens Museum. What was taken?'

With a shake of his head, Michael admitted, 'Just some clothes. Well, one of Charles Dickens' original outfits complete with top hat and walking cane. They seem like odd items for someone to take – I don't see how a person could sell them on.'

'Maybe that is not their intention,' offered Frank.

Michael tilted his head, acknowledging the point. 'What then? They want to play dress up? They were stolen by an aspiring writer who is now wearing them while writing to channel the ghostly spirit of Charles Dickens?' He frowned deeply. 'I met the curator a short while ago, he's a prickly one, for sure. He fired the guard who reported the theft, and I think he did it because he knows something about the crime.'

Frank asked, 'What makes you think that?'

Michael wriggled his lips from side to side as he thought about his answer. 'I more or less accused him and got to see the panic in his eyes. There are lots of cabinets that line the walls with all manner of artefacts displayed, right? So one cabinet is empty because the outfit inside it was stolen, but the cabinets are all sealed and fed by a filtered air system that protects the things inside.' Frank listened patiently, waiting for Michael to make his point. 'Well, the filter system prevents dust forming, or so the curator said but it doesn't remove a hundred percent of it so there was a very fine film on the shelves and it had been disturbed.'

'Someone had been in the other cabinets?' Frank sought clarity.

Michael nodded. 'That's what I think. I wouldn't think

anything of it, but like I said ... the curator acted guilty. Quite how that connects to Ronald Norton going missing, or another shareholder trying to get a loan I have no idea. As for the ghoul ... What do you think?'

Frank rubbed his chin. 'I think we have a ghoul in the area, and no one is dealing with it. That's what I think. Thefts from a museum are not something I care about unless, like you suspect, the two things are somehow linked. The ghoul has claimed our town or at least the local area as its hunting ground and is picking off victims.'

'Just one known victim so far,' Michael countered.

'Well, exactly, *known* is the important word. We don't know about the other victims but if it is eating them and taking from the homeless denizens of the town then we might never know about it.'

Sticking with Frank's rather mad theory, Michael questioned, 'Why then has it taken a prominent and probably rich person? Doesn't that feel like a lot of coincidence to you? The ghoul is sighted at Dickens Greatest Works Theme Park where Ronald Norton is a shareholder. Ronald then goes missing after the park is shut down and was shouting at bank managers because they wouldn't give him a loan.'

A tug at his coat sleeve disturbed what he was going to say next. 'Michael, there are erotic magazines in this store,' reported Mary in a tone that made her disgust clear. 'There are boys looking at them.'

Frank heard her comment, most likely because she intended him to, but explained, 'Those are adult Manga comics. They often depict adult scenes but not in a pornographic manner. They are rated as suitable for minors over the age of twelve.

Mary fixed him with a glare that would have melted

wax. Or possibly steel if she narrowed her eyes just a little more. 'It's disgraceful,' she snapped. 'Filthy,' she added, just in case disgraceful hadn't done it. 'We are leaving right this minute, Michael.'

'But I'm talking to Frank. He says there is a ghoul at the Dickens theme park. I think this is all tied together.' Michael didn't wish to leave just yet. He was getting information. 'I'm on to something here, Mary.'

Mary started for the door where she turned and began to tap her foot with impatience. 'It is not your job, Michael. Leave it to Tempest.'

Michael and Mary had been married for long enough to know to where the other person's limits would stretch. Michael was getting close to his. 'Tempest isn't available, dear,' he replied with false politeness. 'He had something very pressing to deal with. No one is dealing with the crime I have uncovered.'

'Then hand it over to the police,' she growled.

Chief Inspector Quinn

SATURDAY, DECEMBER 24TH 1407HRS

Mary muttered under her breath the whole way to the police station. It was her ill-thought instruction to report his stupid conspiracy theory to the police that meant they were not yet on their way home. She did it to herself and that was the worst of it.

'They won't have time for your nonsense,' she voiced her opinion for the third time. 'Whatever it is you think you know, the police already know it. Trust me.'

'If they knew it, they would be doing something about it,' Michael argued.

Refusing to back down, Mary pointed out, 'You wouldn't know if they were doing something. The police have people who work undercover, do they not?'

He had to concede the point, but he wasn't going to let it go that easily. 'I'm going in, dear.'

'Well don't be long,' Mary griped. 'The three-bird roast is already defrosting.'

Pausing halfway out of the passenger door, Michael grasped the opportunity his wife had just presented. 'Yes, that is a bother. Maybe you should just go home, love. I can walk over the bridge and home when I am done.'

She eyed him suspiciously. 'You won't stop in a pub on the way?'

'Scout's honour.' It was an easy promise to give because he had no intention of going to a pub. He'd noticed that one of the other shareholders lived in Rochester and not too far from the bridge. He could drop in there to ask a few questions on the way home. First though, he was going to do exactly as his wife suggested and talk to the police. He leaned across to kiss her cheek and escaped before she could change her mind.

A final wave saw her back onto the main road where she merged with traffic and vanished from sight. This was much more like it, Michael thought to himself. Michael Michaels, super sleuth and paranormal detective. It had a pleasing ring to it.

It was not the first time he'd ever been to Rochester police station, but he could not remember when he was last here or what it had been for. Searching his memory, he thought it might have been to report a lost wallet. It was insignificant to the matter at hand so he pushed it from his mind and approached the front desk where a young police officer was waiting.

'Good ... afternoon,' he tried, hesitating briefly while he checked the clock behind the man's head. 'I'm here to report ...' What? He was here to report a ghoul and a conspiracy? How did Tempest do this? 'I wondered if it might be possible to speak to someone about the recent theft from the Dickens Museum and the disappearance of Ronald Norton.'

The young male officer looked across at his desk

sergeant and back at Michael Michaels' eyes. 'You wish to confess to the theft?' he queried.

Michael's eyebrows shot to the top of his head. 'Good heavens, no. I wanted to talk to someone about the case because I think I might have spotted a few clues they appear to have missed.'

The desk sergeant, a long looked-over-for-promotion man called Stephens looked up from the report he was writing. It was Christmas Eve for goodness sake; he was expecting crazy people to wander through the door, but not this early in the day.

The young police officer shook his head as if the action would rid him of the confusion he now felt. 'You have spotted some clues?'

'I think so,' Michael replied, not sounding or feeling as confident as he had before he started talking. 'There is a ghoul at the Dickens Greatest Works Theme Park, right?'

'I thought you were talking about the museum,' the officer queried.

'Yes, but also the theme park.' Michael could see he was making a mess of things.

The desk sergeant got to his feet. 'Is this a prank, sir?' He gave the grey-haired gentleman a level stare and folded his arms over his ample belly as a show that he was not impressed. 'Because wasting police time is not taken lightly, sir. I'm sure your family wouldn't like to have you spend the big day in a cell now, would they?'

Tempest's dad could feel heat beginning to radiate from his cheeks. 'I can assure you this is not a prank. I am hoping to assist in the apprehension of a criminal.'

'A ghoul?' Sergeant Stephens repeated the word Michael had himself used. Then made a spooky noise and waved his arms around like a ghost. 'Oooooowwww!'

Feeling his embarrassment and frustration rising, Michael couldn't withdraw the word now, but could defend it. 'A large man, described by those who saw it as a ghoul, has been spotted several times at the Dickens Greatest Works Theme Park.'

'I thought that place closed down?' queried the young officer.

'It did,' Sergeant Stephens assured him. 'Is there anything else, sir? Or would you like to leave now?'

He was being verbally shown the door! Michael Michaels couldn't believe it. 'I came here to help,' he protested. 'There is something going on and a man might be in danger.'

Sergeant Stephens was bored already. 'All right, that's enough. Hop it or I'll arrest you myself.' His face was contorted into an angry threat but rather than make Tempest's dad turn tail, it had the opposite effect.

Just as he was going to lay into the man, a door to Michael's left opened. Several officers in uniform came through it and at the head was a man he recognised.

'Ah, Chief Inspector Quinn. If I might have a word.' Michael turned his back on the unpleasant sergeant, mentally wiping the slate clean and planning to start afresh.

Hearing his name, CI Quinn focussed on the man who had just said it. It took a moment for his mental gears to align, but when they did all he could do was close his eyes and sigh. 'Mr Michaels.'

'Yes, hello.' He'd last seen the chief inspector two days ago. Perhaps, in fact, it was more recent than that because he was leading the police at the old airfield where Tempest managed to finally locate the Undead Incorporated bunch. Before that, he'd seen the chief inspector just outside Reculver where Tempest uncovered a biker gang smuggling illegal immigrants into the country. Michael felt that gave them some common ground.

However, before he could say anything, Sergeant Stephens left the front desk, popping around the back to emerge through another side door. 'He's been in here spouting some nonsense about a ghoul at the Dickens theme park, sir,' he blabbed like a school child ratting another kid out to the teacher.

Chief Inspector Quinn had his own boss right next to him and several other officers of status just behind him. They would all be listening. His record for making big busts had got him a lot of recognition in recent months and he was on track for early promotion to superintendent. They were all going out for a Christmas lunch but now they would be waiting to hear how he dealt with Mr Michaels because they all knew about the man's son and Quinn's association with him.

There were rumours that many of Quinn's successful cases were down to Tempest Michaels actually solving the cases but then stepping aside to let the police make the arrests. It made CI Quinn deeply unhappy, but not as much as finding himself recently forced to hire the Blue Moon Investigation Agency to look into cases with … shall we say, special characteristics. However, he applied some spin to the situation so they then became a tool which he was wielding.

Sucking on his teeth for a second, Quinn turned his attention to the desk sergeant, a slovenly man who was lucky to still have a job in Quinn's opinion. 'Leave this with me, please, Sergeant Stephens. I'll take it from here.'

'Very good, sir.' The sergeant made his way back to his desk and his report, leaving Michael Michaels unsure about where he now stood.

Understanding the importance of perception, Quinn

said, 'I am aware of the reports, Mr Michaels. How may I help you?' Then to the senior officers now waiting for him, he said, 'Gentlemen, please continue without me. I shall be along momentarily.'

Believing he was finally getting somewhere, Michael Michaels did his best to explain the connection between the missing man, the ghoul, and the stolen artefacts.

However, when he finished, Chief Inspector Quinn asked, 'And you believe these elements to be connected somehow?'

Had he explained it poorly? 'Yes. I mean, they must be, right? It's too much for it to be coincidence, surely.'

Chief Inspector Quinn wasn't new to this game, he'd played it many times with the man's son. Holding out an arm to steer the father to the door, he ushered him from the station. 'Mr Michaels, I think you have been overdoing it recently. It has been one thing after another for you with that son of yours. Do you have plans for Christmas?'

Surprised by the change in conversation, he said, 'Yes, but I don't see …'

'I think you should focus on that for now, sir. There is an ongoing investigation into the disappearance of Ronald Norton but no good reason to suspect foul play. There has been no ransom note and his wife suspects him to be having an affair.'

'Did he run off with the other woman?' Michael asked automatically.

They had reached the pavement in front of the station where CI Quinn planned to find out which way Mr Michaels wanted to go and then go the other way, even if it meant a meandering route to get to his own destination. 'That does not appear to be the case; however, I am not treating his disappearance as a priority case. Likewise, the theft from the museum and reports of a ghoul. The latter will turn out to be nothing but shadows and ... given your son's chosen career, I'm surprised you would believe in such a thing.' Michael almost began to argue that he didn't, but what the chief inspector believed was unimportant. 'If you don't mind, Mr Michaels, I really must get along. I have important business to which I must attend.' A very important pint of Christmas beer with his superiors in fact.

'Have there been any other thefts or reports of stolen items from the museum? Do you have someone watching the curator?'

His voice drifted back though he didn't turn his head to answer, 'Have a good Christmas, Mr Michaels.'

Rallying his meagre brain and cursing himself for not being faster, he tried to think of a Christmas comeback that would sting and give him the satisfaction of a well-delivered last line. Something involving Scrooge might work, by the time he'd thought of an idea that might work, the chief inspector was across the road and the moment was gone.

Creeping Suspicions

SATURDAY, DECEMBER 24TH 1422HRS

Blake stopped what he was doing and lifted his head to listen. 'I just heard it again,' he said.

Edward had a piece of cable in his mouth to keep it out of the way as he bared the wires on another cable ready to splice the two. He got that Blake expected him to answer but continued doing what he was doing until he was ready to open his mouth and drop the cable into a hand now that he had one free.

'It's your imagination,' he assured his partner. 'Or it's the wind. We're right on the river.'

Blake frowned. 'It sounds like someone moaning in pain.'

'Just the wind,' persisted Edward. 'It will be catching on something and blowing through it just like a reed instrument. Happens all the time.'

Blake wasn't convinced. The old theme park was giving him the creeps; there were too many unexplained noises and more than once he'd been convinced there was a giant figure watching him from below while he worked. Whenever he looked it was gone and Edward said he hadn't seen anything.

It wasn't like him to jump at shadows but ... something was off with this whole job. 'Do you think he gave in too easily?' Blake asked.

'Are you nearly done?' replied Edward, asking a question with a touch of irritation in his voice. He wanted to get the job done and leave, not waste time questioning the origin of strange noises in an old disused theme park.

'Yes,' Blake answered, absentmindedly as the moaning noise echoed through the building again. 'He said yes to giving us an extra five grand like it was nothing.'

'Maybe it is nothing.' Edward's only issue with the five grand was that he should have asked for ten and was feeling like he cheated himself now.

Blake shook his head. 'Look at this place. There's no money coming in and he's got us rigging explosives to blow a circular hole in the ceiling of the basement. He wouldn't tell us what is above it, would he?'

'So?'

'So he wants us to get the job done and leave. That's what. What if it is something far more valuable than the five grand he agreed to pay us?'

Blake's question made Edward's hands freeze. 'Like what?' he wanted to know, pound signs clicking into place behind his eyes.

Blake shrugged. 'Maybe it's a safe.'

'A safe?' Edward scoffed, but he had to wonder if his partner might be right.

'All right, so maybe it's not a safe. But it must be something, right? You asked for five grand, and he agreed like it was pocket change.'

Edward turned to look at his colleague, a silent

exchange taking place as both men thought about what might be on the floor above them.

They were both sitting on top of a high portable podium, the electric type that scissors up and down to access work at height. On any other site the health and safety squad would have torn them apart and thrown them off site, but they were the only people in the building apart from Mr Dickens. At least, so far as they knew. The moaning sound he kept hearing might be creeping Blake out, but they were about done with the job and that meant they needed to go find Mr Dickens again. One thing was for certain, they were not leaving without their five-grand bonus, but now they were both wondering if there was something far greater at stake.

'We should check it out,' suggested Edward.

'What have you got left to do?'

Edward turned his attention back to the cables in his hands. 'Just connect this up.'

Ten minutes later, the podium had been lowered to the floor, and they were making their way back upstairs to look for Mr Dickens.

Exiting the basement, Edward pointed to their left. 'It's over there somewhere.'

Once they were back on the floor in the basement, they had done their best to estimate the position of the explosives using the walls as reference points. However, upstairs they were in the theme park and the walls were hidden from sight. That made it hard to pinpoint where they wanted to go and the lights being off didn't help. Nevertheless, they had a rough idea and discovered that where they believed the ring of explosives to be was behind a wall.

They followed it until they found a way in, both pausing

beneath the entrance to read the sign above their head. 'The Dickens experience flume ride,' Edward said aloud.

Venturing inside, it was quickly clear they were blowing up a section of floor beneath the ride. It was impossible to pinpoint the exact location, though Mr Dickens had already marked it out for them on the ceiling below so he must have worked it out.

'Why are we blowing up an old theme park flume ride?' asked Blake.

He didn't expect an answer and didn't get one. Instead, Edward said, 'Let's just hope that Mr Dickens gets back here soon with the money, this place gives me the creeps. Here, do you fancy a pint at the Drowned Duck before you head home? I'm buying.'

The House of Richard Glaagard

SATURDAY, DECEMBER 24TH 1454HRS

Using his new-fangled phone, Michael managed to find the contact number he had for Rob Whittaker, the guard from the museum who he knew from the veterans' bar. However, when he made the phone call it went directly to voice mail.

'Rob, this is Michael Michaels. Can you call me back? It's about the thefts from the museum.' Message left, he thought about calling Mary but dismissed the idea. If she knew he was finished at the police station she would expect him home. This way, unless she directly asked him what time he had left, he could bluff that he came from there to her. He wasn't taking that much of a detour though, just going the long route to check on something.

The walk took Michael longer than he expected which was mostly because he couldn't find the house he was looking for. He ignored it the first two times he passed it because, to his mind, it wasn't a house. It registered on his mental scale for houses as a residence, which placed it one above a property and one below a grand mansion. Having finally spotted the name on the plaque outside, he then questioned whether he should be approaching the front door even as he wandered along the sweeping driveway.

Glaagard Point overlooked the river Medway from a commanding position not far from the castle. It was a tall, wide, imposing building that did not look inviting at all. Perhaps in the summer months when there were leaves on the trees and bushes and flowers growing in the beds it would have a more appealing front façade.

However, there were Christmas lights flashing in the window, and a tree visible in a ground floor window, its brightly coloured decorations easy to see as Michael approached the house. There were cars too, several of them, including a rather nice Italian sports car.

To the left as he looked at the property, was a carport and garage that looked capable of housing several cars. To the right were trees and bushes, clipped and shaped to show that the garden was well-tended by someone. Just as he was admiring the shrubbery, Michael saw a face move in and out of the greenery.

Jolting him like an electric shock, Michael's pulse immediately spiked as if he'd been caught doing something very wrong. Remembering that he was just a person walking down a driveway to a house, he forced his feet to continue and stared into the spot where the face had been.

It appeared again, just a small portion of it, but closer now Michael was able to see it more clearly and his blood ran cold.

Unless the man was standing on a ladder it had to be the tallest person Michael had ever seen. Its face was deathly pale, and it had a broken top hat perched on its skull. The hat looked almost comical because it was far too small for the head on which it rested. Michael had been moving forward but his next step faltered as fear drove a spike through his heart and froze him to the spot.

He was looking right at the ghoul.

There was no question in Michael's mind, but even though the face he saw terrified him, he told himself it was just a man. He even said it out loud, 'It's just a man, Michaels. Get a grip.' With an annoyed growl at himself, when the face ducked back into the bushes, he broke into a run.

The greenery ahead rustled and swayed as it would if someone were forcing their way through it. The movement was going away from him, suggesting the ghoul had chosen to flee. Nevertheless, Michael was running toward potential danger and he was already questioning his sanity. He might have done it without thinking forty or even thirty years ago, but closing in fast on his seventieth birthday, he no longer possessed the physicality to deal with whatever he might find if it chose to put up a fight. That wasn't going to deter him though. He'd watched Tempest and his giant friend, Big Ben, wade in against superior numbers and come out on top and he wasn't going to let his own imagination beat him before he found out if there was even something to be scared of.

Fear of the unknown did slow his feet as he reached the bushes though. Plunging blindly into them was just a little too foolhardy since the ghoul could have easily doubled back and be waiting to ambush him.

Peering into the greenery, he found nothing and pushed through the tall shrubs and around small trees employing a degree of caution. Dampness on the foliage clung to his clothes, making his trousers wet. His coat, too, though it hardly mattered. The shrubs were thick and not designed for people to pass between. However, they were not deep and clear space appeared beyond them no sooner than Michael lost the clear space behind. He emerged to find he was at the side of the house. Windows to his left were above his head, the building stretching on for a hundred feet or more where it met a wall with a door to lead into what he assumed was a garden beyond.

His breathing came in lumps, his body shocked by the sudden and unexpected burst of energy. Clouds of vapour formed above his head as he paused to look around. There was nothing Michael could see to indicate which way the ghoul might have gone, though when he looked, he spotted what appeared to be a fresh mark on the frost-covered ground.

To his right, the space ended at a low wall perhaps three feet high. Bordering it, and about four feet deep, was a herb garden that had all but died back to nothing. The rosemary, hardy beast that it is, still stood strong against the elements but leafier herbs were gone, leaving nothing but ornate labels to show where they had once been. At the corner of the herb garden, weeds and grass had taken hold and it was there in the thick coating of frost that he could see someone had left a footprint.

Feeling like a detective as he approached it, Michael's eyes widened of their own accord: the footprint was massive. It wasn't a full print, but the toes and front half of the sole. He mimed the motion of running, proving to himself that if he were sprinting, he would leave the same mark. Hovering his foot above the mark to get a sense of size, his could only snort at how small his own shoe was by comparison.

Sudden noises coming from the front of the house sounded like the electronic squelch sound one gets from radios. It was quickly followed by the sound of voices and then by the shrubs rustling as someone/something forced its way through.

Expecting it to be the police, and jolly glad too since he hadn't had the presence of mind to call them himself, he smiled when two officers in uniform burst into sight. They were both young men in their twenties, and both producing clouds of vapour as they ran toward him.

'C'mon, chaps,' he shot them a wave. 'I think he went this way!' With the police here now, he felt reinvigorated and was running across the herb garden to get to the low wall.

'Don't move!'

The shout came from behind him, making him spin around to see who they were talking to. 'Excuse me?' Michael had enough time to raise his eyebrows and then he was tackled to the ground. 'What the heck! I'm not the one you want! I was chasing …' he almost said the word ghoul but held off as he remembered what had happened at the police station. His arms were yanked roughly behind his back and cold steel bit into his wrists as a pair of cuffs snapped home. He didn't resist; there was no point, but he did continue to talk. 'I'm telling you; you've just let the person you want get away. While you waste your time with me, he is making good his escape.

The officers helped Michael to his feet, one of them using his radio to talk to someone else, 'Yes, we've got him. He tried to run. We'll bring him back around to the front of the house.'

His partner turned Michael around so they were facing each other. 'Are you armed, sir?'

'What? No,' Michael huffed a breath out through his nose, frustrated that they were refusing to listen.

Not taking his word for it, the cop patted him down

anyway, tapping down his coat and then his trousers, stopping at his left hip pocket. 'What's this?' he asked, tapping a hard lump.

With a sigh, Michael said, 'A pocketknife.'

'Gaz, he's carrying a knife,' the cop advised his partner.

Both cops eyed him critically. Surely, they could see he wasn't a criminal. He was smartly dressed and in his late sixties for goodness sake. They gripped his arms though, one either side to frog march him the long way around the shrubs to get back to the front of the house where two more cops were waiting. At the far end of the drive were two squad cars, their roof lights lazily spinning.

Getting closer, he realised he recognised one of them, a short, black woman he'd seen with Tempest and Amanda a few times. Fixing what he hoped was an innocent smile to his face, Michael said, 'Hello.'

Constable Patience Woods had just a few hours of her shift left and she had a full two days off. She was going to enjoy them and was thinking about nothing else at all. She was going to eat and drink and be merry. However, rather than having a quiet relaxing day before Christmas, it had been surprisingly busy with various silly calls, including this one where the owner of a huge house reported a strange man lurking outside his house. The owner was hiding inside with his wife and children.

It pleased her greatly when Gaz and Marco radioed to say they'd found him because she had eaten too many mince pies for lunch and wasn't feeling up to chasing anyone right now. But when they reappeared, they had a retirement age gentleman with them, and as he came closer, he smiled at her and spoke.

It took a second, but she realised she knew him. 'Mr Michaels?'

'Hello,' Michael repeated, racking his brain to remember the lady's name.

'You know this man, Patience?' Gaz asked.

That was it: Patience. 'I've been trying to tell them they have the wrong man, Patience. They don't seem to want to listen,' Michael lamented.

'He was carrying a knife,' Gaz held up a clear plastic bag with a small, red Swiss army knife inside.

'It's just a tool,' Michael told them for the third time.

The front door to the house opened, the sound drawing their eyes. A man in his forties with short-cut blonde hair and Scandinavian features appeared in the gap with two small children peering around his legs. 'Who's that?' he asked, nodding his head toward Michael Michaels.

'Are you the owner of the house, sir?' asked Patience, hoping they could clear this up quickly and get back into their nice warm squad cars. She had a salted caramel hot chocolate in hers and it was going to go cold if they didn't hurry up.

The man spoke to his children, ushering them back inside and closing the door behind him as he made his way outside. He had on one of those garish Christmas jumpers; the sort of garment that one's wife buys and thus one had to wear until the holiday season is over and it can be accidentally lost in the dustbin forever. Tucking his hands under his armpits and hugging himself against the cold, he replied, 'Yes. I'm Richard Glaagard. I'm the one who called you. Who is this man?'

Beating the cops to it, Michael said, 'I'm Michael Michaels. I'm investigating what might have happened to Ronald Norton. He is a business partner of yours, I believe. I have reason to believe he was taken by someone and came here to warn you. Approaching your house, I spotted a large man lurking in the bushes. He saw me and ran. I gave chase but he got away.'

It was the most complete report the police had heard from him thus far and it caused several questions to emerge in rapid fire. Chief among which came from Patience, who said, 'You called us about a prowler. Is this the man you saw?'

Richard Glaagard shook his head. 'No, the man I saw was much taller and he was wearing a top hat.'

'That's who I saw,' confirmed Michael.

'He was carrying a knife,' pointed out Gaz once more, unable to let his one point go.

Patience frowned at him. 'That's hardly a knife, Gaz. Its blade is clearly less than two and a half inches, so it doesn't count. Take the cuffs off and let him have it back.'

Smiling gamely, Michael waggled his eyebrows when he caught Patience's eye. 'There's a footprint around the side of the house. It's twice the size of mine.'

Feeling sad about her hot chocolate, Patience said, 'I guess we had better take a look.'

A New Plan

SATURDAY, DECEMBER 24TH 1502HRS

The man calling himself Mr Dickens was once again wearing his fancy frock coat though the Charles Dickens mask came off as soon as he started the engine. At the wheel of a silver van and driving along the esplanade toward Rochester bridge he had to fight hard to control his rage. He had a tiny window to grab his last three victims and one had just slipped through his fingers. Richard Glaagard was one of those he wanted most. Glaagard had been vocal in damning the plans for expansion at the theme park. Unlike Jason Pendergrass, who always had something better to do, Richard came to the shareholder meetings, but where this ought to have been a positive opportunity for interaction, Mr Dickens found that Richard Glaagard just wanted to stamp on his proposals and make it impossible for the park to advance.

His plans had been pure brilliance; no one would ever convince him otherwise. They entrusted him with taking the theme park forward but then could not understand that such things take time. They wanted immediate returns on their investment – some now, not lots later as he proposed.

The man calling himself Mr Dickens was going to show Glaagard, but how was he going to grab him now? Silently seething in the driver's seat of the van, he glanced in the rear-view mirror to see the ghoul hunched up in the back. He was too distinctive to have in the front of the van, but he was also too big to fit into the seat anyway.

There had been still two more shareholders to get if the ghoul had been successful in grabbing Glaagard, but now it was three. When the ghoul came running back through the bushes, Dickens caught a glimpse of the old man following him – he wasn't police, and he didn't look like he was part of Glaagard's family. So who was he?

Dickens pushed it from his thoughts to concentrate on the next task: grabbing Mason Sabre. Mason was going to be the easy one. He lived at home in a big, detached place with no neighbours that could see in. The ghoul would grab Mason when he answered the door. It still left Glaagard and Cudmore, but as his frustration cooled, and he allowed himself some time to think clearly, a plan presented itself.

A small smile tugged one corner of his mouth. It was a little theatrical, but there was no harm in that. The danger was in the need to take the ghoul out in public. It might be tricky, but if he chose the right location, one that would not alert his intended victims or make them feel overly trepidatious, then he felt certain he could still pull this off. The new plan might even be better, but that was the kind of man he was – one who never saw a problem, only an opportunity.

Everything was going to work out perfectly.

Trouble with Mary

SATURDAY, DECEMBER 24TH 1525HRS

The sound of Michael's phone ringing broke through the still air of the winter's day. Mr Glaagard had gone back inside to fetch a coat but was with them as they all followed Michael around to the side of the house. Patience had used the brief interlude while they waited for the homeowner to explain who Michael was or, rather, who his son was. They all knew the name Tempest Michaels; it was almost impossible not to because his face, and that of their former police colleague Amanda Harper, had been splashed across the local newspapers, and indeed the national press, several times in the recent months.

Whether the male officers were impressed or not, Michael couldn't tell but they were certainly acting like they didn't care. They were following him so they could see the footprint because it was their job to do so. The homeowner reported a prowler and described him as disturbing looking though Mr Glaagard also said he wasn't able to get a good look at the man at any point.

Sensing an opportunity, Michael hung back to walk with the museum shareholder, but his phone rang before he got the chance to speak. He cringed as he reached into his pocket because he knew which name would be displayed on the screen. He knew because Tempest had helped him assign a ringtone a while back and the sound of Darth Vader's Imperial March cutting through the chill air was hard to mistake for anything else.

'Hello, dear,' Michael tried, putting emphatic joy into his voice as if hearing hers could lift his spirits so.

He could almost feel her annoyed expression when she replied, 'Don't you go "Hello Dearing" me, Michael Michaels. You've been gone ages, and you promised me you wouldn't go to the pub.'

'Well, dear I would have been home already, but I am assisting the police with their enquiries at the moment.'

'No, you're not! Don't you dare lie to me. Tell me the truth right now!' Mary Michaels had always been a difficult one to convince once she'd decided she knew what was happening.

Huffing a breath that ruffled his lips, Michael held up the phone and called out, 'Constable Woods? Any chance you could have just a very brief word with my wife? She thinks I'm off galivanting or something.'

He pressed the button to engage the speaker and held the phone out so Patience could talk. 'Hello. Is this Mrs Michaels? This is Constable Patience Woods. I think we might have met once, but I'm not sure. I know your son anyw …'

Mary interrupted her. 'No.'

Patience jinked an eyebrow. 'No?'

'No,' Mary repeated. 'You're some trollop in the pub

that's he's got talking to. I've never heard of a Patience Woods. Tell that idiot husband of mine he's to get himself home right now or ...'

Whatever she said next went unheard as Michael stabbed the speaker button once more to disengage it and put the phone back to his ear. The police officers were all close enough to hear what his wife had said and were smirking at him now.

'Hello again, dear. If you want me home, please come to this address.' He recited where they were. 'You'll find me there with several police officers who I *am* helping with their enquiries. I have to go; there's a criminal at large.' He cut the call off with a satisfactory stab of the red button.

The call filled the gap between moving from the front of the house to the side where the police officers were now fanning out to inspect the ground. The footprint was easy to see, not least because Michael pointed it out to them. Hanging back, he grabbed his chance to ask Mr Glaagard some questions.

'Were you aware Ronald Norton had gone missing?'

Richard nodded. 'I saw the article in the paper. Actually, it was my wife who saw it and pointed it out to me. You say you think something might have happened to him rather than he just took off?'

Michael didn't wish to overstate the case but believed something screwy was going on. 'There are a number of factors which all seem to correlate. What was your relationship like with him?'

Glaagard flipped a mental coin as he tried to decide whether to tell the old man to stop asking questions but figured it couldn't do any harm to provide a few details. 'We didn't get along. Why do you ask?'

Michael let a breath go as he ran the clues through his head. 'Why? Because my gut tells me he was taken and the presence of the …' he almost said *ghoul*, 'prowler here earlier leads me to believe the same might have been about to happen to you. Things have been stolen from the museum, the curator was acting cagey when I asked him about it, and I saw Norton myself last week. He was in the bank shouting at the manager because they wouldn't give him a loan. Do you know why he would need a loan? Surely, he was well off if he was a shareholder.'

Richard Glaagard eyed the older man dubiously, wondering why he was involved, but again chose to answer his question. 'Ronald Norton got his shares because he was the CEO of the theme park. He never received a dividend from them though because he chose to run the place into the ground. He is the chief reason it failed and closed.'

This was news to Michael. 'He ran the theme park?'

'Into the ground, yes,' remarked Glaagard. 'I wanted him out, but the others – other shareholders that is – were fooled by his plans for development. He is a very charismatic man, I guess that's why we hired him, but the job proved too much. He was supposed to invest our money in new attractions and in marketing the theme park, but he set out on a ten-year plan he failed to tell us about. It involved taking our money and buying all the properties around the existing theme park's footprint. He wanted to spend billions making the park into some kind of British Disney World, but there was just no guarantee of success. When I found out, I cut his plans off at the knees. I thought we were going to lose the whole investment – the park was failing because of his lack of management. It turned out, though, that the land is worth a fortune. He did us a big favour, though that was never his intention. It's about to be sold and will be turned into riverside apartments. The shareholders will get all their money back, even Ronald will get a payout.'

'Because he is also a shareholder?' Michael Michaels found the whole premise confusing.

Glaagard nodded. 'It was part of his package. He got a small number of shares. That's fairly typical for chief executives as it keeps them incentivised and links their pay directly to performance.'

'Why was he after a loan?'

Michael got a shrug in response. 'That I could not hope to guess, Mr Michaels. He lost his job when we closed the theme park, perhaps he has been unable to find new employment and is in need of financial assistance.'

Spotting a possible motivation for events, Michael asked, 'Did he hold a grudge?' When Glaagard hitched an eyebrow, Michael clarified, 'Against you for wanting him out?'

One of the police officers had found something over at the wall. It drew Mr Glaagard's attention, and he set off to see what it was. As he walked away, he said, 'I can assure you the man I saw today was not Ronald Norton.'

Michael Michaels stayed where he was, unsure what to do next. He was onto something, he felt sure of that, but he couldn't get anyone to listen. Not even the police.

What the cops found was a handprint in the frost adhered to the top of the wall. The ghoul had vaulted the wall placing his left hand on top as he went over. There was a drop of about eight feet the other side. Enough to make Michael question whether he would have vaulted it himself.

On a different day, when the clouds cleared to let the sun shine through, the frost would have been long gone, but the cool temperatures and low cloud cover meant it had lingered. Together with the footprint, it gave them all an indication for the size of the individual they were dealing with.

Patience whistled a low sound of appreciation. 'That is one big handprint. I bet a basketball looks like a walnut in a hand that size.'

Shareholders

SATURDAY, DECEMBER 24TH 1605HRS

Christmas Eve traffic was heavy it seemed which had two effects. The first of which was that it took Mary far longer than expected to get to him, by which time Michael was getting cold and needed the toilet. The second was that Mary was hopping mad.

'I've spent half the day in the car,' she pointed out. 'It took me twenty minutes just to get to the bridge.'

Sympathising, Michael said, 'Oh dear. Yes, it can get a little clogged sometimes.'

Mary wanted to poke him in the hip with a fork. 'Are you ready to go?' she enquired, trying to focus on the glass of sherry she poured but didn't get to taste before she found she needed to go out again to collect her ridiculous husband.

He looked about. 'Yes, dear. I think so.' The cops were waiting for a forensics team to arrive. Richard Glaagard had latched onto Michael's idea that he or his family might be in danger and was making enough noise to cause the police to take the matter seriously. The recent disappearance of Ronald Norton played a big part in that.

Whatever the forensics team might find, it was out of Michael's hands and he was cold enough now to happily head for home. Walking to the car, Mary reminded him about all the things he still needed to do before they could go out tonight – they wouldn't want to do it when they got home from the performance and they wouldn't have time in the morning.

Michael kept quiet while she berated him. That is until she asked, 'What is that on your coat? It looks like makeup.'

He tried to follow where her eyes were looking, turning his head around to the right but she was indicating a point on the back of his arm in line with his shoulder blade.

'Hold still,' Mary insisted as she came in close to grab his sleeve. Pulling at it, she scraped with her fingernail and held it up. 'No, it's not makeup, at least, not a woman's. I don't know what it is, but you have a line of it along your sleeve like you wiped it on something. You'll have to take it off before you get in the car.'

He was already cold; taking his coat off did not appeal, but there was no option that Michael could see. Inside the car, he used the coat as a blanket over his legs and lower half since the lining was warm from his body heat. It also meant the back of his coat now faced him, and he could inspect the 'makeup' for himself.

It was a creamy thick paste like coloured Vaseline. There wasn't much of it, just a thin line but it would have marked the car's upholstery as Mary said.

Traffic flowing over the bridge into Strood was slow but moving, unlike the traffic going the other way which did not look to be moving much at all. The journey took double the time it normally would, but still only about ten minutes. It was long enough for Michael to ponder what he had seen so far today.

Once home, he dutifully set about packing a small suitcase before Mary had a chance to remind him to do so. She was downstairs in her usual chair, knitting and singing along to more God-awful Cliff Richard. That she tended to play it loud helped in many ways because it drowned out her singing, however today it had an added bonus – she wouldn't be able to hear him making phone calls.

The suitcase was on the bed, shorts and socks thrown in haphazardly because the task was performed at speed. Sitting next to it, he fished out the pages printed at the library and shuffled them until he got to the shareholders. He called Elizabeth Cudmore first and ran through what he wanted to say while it rang.

'Hello?' the voice that answered the phone was female, middle-aged and posh. Elizabeth Cudmore was in the habit of pronouncing her words correctly, thank you very much.

Michael took a breath and started speaking. 'Good afternoon, Mrs Cudmore. First let me please assure you that I am not calling to sell you anything. My name is Michael Michaels, and I am an investigator.'

A beat of silence followed while downstairs Cliff warbled about mistletoe and wine, and Michael thought the lady might be about to hang up. 'What is it that you are investigating, Mr Michaels?' Mrs Cudmore asked.

Okay, he'd made it past the awkward cold call introduction. 'Mrs Cudmore are you aware that Ronald Norton recently went missing?'

'Yes, what of it?' She wasn't exactly short with him, but she made it clear she wanted him to get to the point.

That made it easier. 'Ronald Norton is missing, items have been stolen from the Dickens Museum for which you are still a shareholder, and Richard Glaagard had a prowler at his house just a short while ago.' He made the point about the prowler last on purpose. 'I have reason to believe that you and the other shareholders may be in some danger.'

'Danger?' Mrs Cudmore's voice did not contain any sign of concern, if anything, she sounded as if she wanted to laugh at the idea. 'Why would we be in any danger? Who from?'

'That I do not yet know, Mrs Cudmore,' Michael admitted reluctantly. 'I wish I did, but the circumstances of Ronald Norton's disappearance are such that I am led to believe he was taken. I was with Mr Glaagard earlier and caught a glimpse of the prowler so I can assure you the danger is real.'

'So you called to warn me?' she concluded.

Michael sucked on his teeth for a second. 'That and to check that you were unharmed at this time. Also, I hoped to ask you some questions.'

Mrs Cudmore tutted. 'You'll have to make it quick, Mr Michaels, I have my family here and we are all getting ready to go to the castle. There is a big open-air play there tonight.'

Michael didn't mention that he was going as well, instead doing as instructed and getting to the questions. He quizzed her about animosity between the shareholders, whether there were any employees who took the park closing personally or voiced a grudge at the time. Had people been paid or were the staff still owed wages when they were released. She took afront to the suggestion that the theme park owners might have skipped out owing pay to the employees, and he apologised, but he was learning fast now. Unfortunately, what he was learning didn't get him anywhere.

When Mrs Cudmore insisted she had to go, Michael knew she had been generous with her time and thanked her genuinely. The call ended and he tried Mason Sabre, the next shareholder on the list. However, his phone came up as 'caller busy'. Michael wasn't entirely clear on how the new mobile phones worked but had seen people on television shows put one call on hold to answer another. If Mason Sabre knew how to do that, he was choosing not to, so Michael ended the call and tried the next name: Jason Pendergrass.

His phone just rang until it went to voicemail. At which point Michael left a message.

What Michael didn't know was that his voice message was heard, not by Jason Pendergrass but by the man who now had his phone and who was about to send a message to Mason Sabre.

More Guests to the Party

SATURDAY, DECEMBER 24TH 1647HRS

'Who is Michael Michaels?'

Jason Pendergrass swallowed hard. His mouth was parched from being without water all day. He was also freezing cold and still tied up with his hands behind his back. That the man in the Dickens outfit with the awful mask planned him harm was for certain and the thought of dying in this musty, dark room made him want to wet himself in terror.

'I don't know,' Jason managed to stammer. 'I've never heard of him.'

Mr Dickens eyed Jason carefully, looking for a lie. The voicemail message *had* sounded like the man was introducing himself. Whoever he was, he claimed to be a private investigator which meant he wasn't a police officer and thus probably nothing to worry about. Was that right though? Shouldn't he worry? Michael Michaels had pieced enough parts together to know to call Jason Pendergrass, and he said he'd spoken to some of the other shareholders. "Call me back as a matter of urgency, please." That was how the message ended. It was clear he didn't know much; he hadn't worked out how the pieces should fit together, but he might if given enough time.

A random thought occurred to him as he remembered the old man at Glaagard's house. Could that have been Michael Michaels? Whether it was or wasn't, he was going to have to deal with him. He had an easy way to do that, but it would have to wait because he was too close to finishing his grand work now.

Jason watched as the man dressed as Charles Dickens came out of his crouch, standing up again and taking a step back. To his great horror, the man who refused to give his name, said, 'Ghoul.' The giant, lumbering menace came into view, clumping around the corner in his enormous boots to stand at his master's shoulder. 'I think it's time we moved Mr Pendergrass into position. Take him to the boat.'

Overwhelmed with terror, Jason still managed to buck and shout as the huge creature came for him. His cries for help echoed off the walls and ceiling in the confined space but no one answered or gave any indication they might have heard.

'You shouldn't waste your breath, dear fellow,' the ghoul's master chuckled. 'There isn't a live soul that can hear you.'

The ghoul grabbed Jason with two giant hands, hauling him from the floor like he weighed nothing and threw him over one shoulder like a sack of flour. They were leaving the room, which pleased Jason, and he was getting some transferred warmth from the ghoul's body, which was a relief because it meant the creature wasn't dead even though he looked it. However, as they came out of the room, he saw where he was.

'Hey, we're at the theme park,' he blurted. He recognised the place because he'd been given a tour when the opportunity to invest arose. A couple of the other investors, Glaagard and that chap that looked like a rat, Mason Sabre, had both insisted they wanted to see everything. They wanted to be certain about what they were buying into. It hadn't stopped them from losing a pile of money before they pulled the plug though. It was a small mercy the idiot running the place had bought land with their investment because they were about to get their money back. That was blind luck though.

Jason was about to ask why they were in the basement beneath the theme park when his breath caught in his throat. Lying on the ground against the side of the wall were two young men in construction worker gear. They looked like they were both very dead. One's head was facing the wrong way so the back of his skull was in line with the vee of his fluorescent vest. Jason almost vomited down the ghoul's back when the sight made him heave.

He couldn't take his eyes from it, but mercifully they left it behind as the ghoul followed his master. Unfortunately, they then passed a third man lying on the floor, this one tall and thin and wearing a suit. His head was on sideways so that his left ear was touching his left shoulder and this time Jason saw that he knew who it was: Professor Loughborough the museum curator.

There was no question the man was dead, but who would want to hurt a museum curator?

Stairs brought them to the next floor which again Jason recognised. They were passing the interactive feature where an animatronic Charles Dickens told extracts from his greatest novels. Coming up on the right would be the flume ride if Jason's memory held true.

He was correct but hadn't expected them to go into it. When the ghoul's master said they were going to the boat, he figured there would be an actual boat. He'd been able to smell the river even in his dungeon.

The man dressed as Dickens started talking again. 'I'm afraid there will be a hiatus before the ride can get started. I need to collect another couple of guests yet. Not to worry though, you'll have company now. Not that you'll be able to talk, of course. I can't have you cooking up some hair-brained escape plan, now can I?'

The ghoul stopped, and with a shrug of his shoulder, bounced Jason from it to catch him just as his feet hit the floor. They were inside the ride at the point where visitors would climb aboard the boats to sail around a nineteenth century Kentish village as depicted in so many of Charles Dickens greatest works. One of the four-seater wooden boats was waiting to depart and in the back seat was another man.

'Mason Sabre,' murmured Jason, recognising him instantly. He looked dishevelled, and his eyes were wide with panic or horror. Like Jason, he was tied up, but also gagged and tied to a lashing point that had been added to the boat between his feet.

The ghoul's master nodded, the unspoken instruction clear to the ghoul who hefted Jason painfully by his arms and dropped him into the boat next to Mason.

Jason bucked and struggled again, not wanting to have his binding attached to the ship. Was the plan to sink them on the ride and watch them drown? Why? The ghoul produced a piece of cloth from a pocket and moved in to apply a gag. With a chance to blurt one last question, Jason chose, 'Why are you doing this?'

The ghoul's master held up a hand to stay his giant pet. 'To help you understand,' cooed the mad man. 'Mason knows why, of course. He recognises my voice, don't you, Mason?'

Mason couldn't answer but blinked his terrified eyes and mumbled something unintelligible.

'It was all so avoidable,' Mr Dickens lamented. 'None of this had to happen, but once I have the last two shareholders, I have a nice presentation for you that explains everything.'

Another nod caused the ghoul to grab Jason's head. He tried to fight but it was like trying to shove a mountain and he had no arms. When the ghoul put a massive hand around his throat and squeezed, Jason stopped fighting and let him apply the gag. Then he used a plastic zip tie to connect his bindings to another lashing eye in the bottom of the boat. With both men secure, the ghoul stepped back onto the shore.

'Here is the clever part, Mr Pendergrass,' said the ghoul's master. 'You are going to be the one to help me get Elizabeth and Richard. I'm sure they will be happy to meet you when you send them an urgent text message.' The man pulled Jason's phone from one of his fine Victorian coat pockets and proceeded to use it, chatting amiably as he did. 'I just happen to know that Elizabeth will be at the big Christmas Eve production at the castle this evening. You'd think doing *A Christmas Carol* year after year would wear people down, but they seem to come in droves,' he chuckled. 'Still, it will make a convenient location for 'you' to meet with them, don't you think?'

Neither man could answer, and it seemed their opinion wasn't really of interest, for the man in the mask turned without another word and left them in the boat. The ghoul trudged after his master and a few seconds later all the lights went out and the footsteps faded away. The two captives were left with nothing but the sound of their own breathing and the gentle lapping of the water.

Open Air Theatre

SATURDAY, DECEMBER 24TH 1722HRS

A flash lit the air with an accompanying whoosh sound that drew eyes and heads. Another firework exploded in the sky above the castle, helping to entice the crowds in. Many had tickets, such as Michael and Mary but they could be bought at ticket booths dotted around the various entrances to the grounds just as easily.

The grey blanket of clouds had moved away, dropping the temperature a few more degrees which made it really quite cold, but there were portable heaters belting out warm air and lots of vendors selling warm drinks and hot food. Mary wanted a mulled wine and a bag of roasted chestnuts but saw no need to queue for such things herself. She wanted to get a good seat, so they apportioned the tasks, Michael agreeing to get the food and drink while Mary arranged herself on one of the benches with the blankets they had brought along.

He had to admit that the Christmas Eve stage production, tired story though it was, had a certain romantic flair to it and the setting was hard to beat. Spotlights highlighted the ancient castle ruins which towered above them while yet more lights were set high and aimed downward to illuminate the stage from above. The players were not yet visible but an orchestra, there to give ambience and mood when required could be heard warming up.

All around them happy people were out as couples or families. Something close to half of all the people attending had dressed for the occasion, as was the tradition. Clad in fancy Victorian outfits, it gave the event a certain extra something. Were Mary to ever suggest dressing up, he would go along with it, but she never had.

The queue for the mulled wine was a long one as was that for the chestnuts, but Michael had seen other vendors just outside the castle grounds so headed back to the entrance they'd recently come through. He still had his ticket for re-entry so timing his exit to slip through a break in the tide of people coming in, he snuck out and found the queues this side were significantly shorter.

Determining that the wine would lose its temperature more swiftly, he joined the queue for the chestnuts first. There were only a few people in front of him and they were being moved along quickly - one person continually tossing and turning the chestnuts, the next bagging them and a third handing them over to hungry customers in a slick process. He took two bags, pocketing them and liking the warmth they imparted through his coat.

He didn't make it to the mulled wine stall.

The castle sits on raised ground near the river so standing just outside the outer wall, he had a view down over the open plaza in front of the cathedral and to North Gate where the city entrance once lay. Along Epaul Lane, opposite the Boley Hill car park entrance is an alleyway. If a person were to look on a map, it shows the alley as a dead end, but it isn't, it just narrows to a choke point that a person can fit through, but only just. In the light coming through from the High Street on the other side, a silhouette stood out. It was only there for a second, but it was unmistakeable to Michael's eyes because a second shadow standing far too close gave it perspective.

The second shadow was a normal height and size human being. The first one was not, and it had hold of the second one by the throat.

It was the ghoul again, made unmistakable not only by its enormous height but also by the broken top hat perched on its head.

Michael was seeing it in silhouette, the image like one of those Chinese theatre puppet shows done with pieces of card. His feet had automatically taken him forward a few steps, getting him a yard or so closer though he was still most of fifty yards away.

Witness to an attack that no one else appeared to have seen, his heart started beating at many times its usual speed. He started forward, then stopped. What was he proposing to do? The ghoul - he figured he might as well call it that even though he felt certain it was just a man - presented a threat he knew he could not overcome, so what did he do? Walk away? Get the wine and watch the show with Mary?

He started running, looking around for security or a cop, and yelling as he ran down Castle Hill. 'Hey! Hey, everyone look! Someone is being attacked!' Michael ran but no one came with him. He got a few strange looks, but nothing more.

There wasn't a police officer in sight, but he spotted a

pair of event security guards on their way back from a stand of portaloos. Diverting his route slightly, Michael yelled at them, 'Guys, there's someone being attacked in the alley. Come on.'

Both men looked at him but neither moved to follow. It forced him to turn around to look at them, running sideways as he shouted again. 'You're security! Move your butts!' Reluctantly, they followed, arguing between themselves that this was not what they were employed for and asking where the police were.

Arriving in the mouth of the alley, Michael was just in time to see the huge, menacing ghoul lift a lifeless body from the cobbles. It made his blood run cold and caused his feet to stop. He had no weapon, and little chance of beating the enormous beast even if he did.

The security guards, still arguing that they needed to get back to managing the crowd, also came into the alley, at which point they turned tail and ran, yelling expletives as they beat a retreat.

Light coming from behind the ghoul meant Michael could not see its features. He couldn't see much at all except for the silhouette it cast. The body hung from one enormous hand, inert and lifeless but clearly that of a man. No one was moving, Michael because he was all but petrified, and the ghoul just stood there facing him as if waiting for its next instruction.

Michael's breath came in ragged gasps, the short run once again shocking his body and he felt weak from the adrenalin. How was it that no one was coming to his aid? He had shouted blue murder and surely the security guards were alerting people. But Michael knew the nature of people: they would ignore a situation if they could and make excuses to themselves afterward. Someone would come, the police probably, but Michael didn't think they would get to him before he had to decide what to do about the ghoul and his victim.

Then, a third shadow appeared next to the ghoul, detaching itself from a wall where it had remained unnoticed until it chose to move. This one was the size and height of a normal man. He wore a dapper coat which hung to his knees and a top hat though his looked to be new, not old, battered, and broken like the ghoul's. In his right hand, a walking cane could be seen, and Michael knew what he was looking at.

'Hey, that's the outfit that was stolen from the Dickens Museum,' he blurted. Looking back, he decided it wasn't the coolest line ever spoken to a master criminal upon first meeting, but he didn't get to reflect on it at the time because the third shadow spoke.

'Michael Michaels? Do I have that right?' Michael had no idea who the man was or how he knew his name, and he didn't get a chance to ask because the man decided he was right and said, 'Get him too.'

The ghoul opened his hand, dropping his victim to the cobbles where it landed with a thud. Then, to Michael's horror, it started coming his way. In the dark recesses of his brain, Michael knew this was precisely the right time to deploy the killer line. Unfortunately, the only neurons firing were the ones telling him he needed to develop the power of flight, not think up cool retorts.

Behind the ghoul, the man in Charles Dickens clothes began to drag the body along the cobbles, but Michael couldn't worry about that right now because the ghoul had broken into a run.

Lumbering might be a more accurate word, but

however you describe it, he was now coming for Michael Michaels and that made him want to be somewhere else. He wasn't one for screaming in terror. He could not remember having done so at any point in his life and felt fairly certain his son, Tempest, would do precisely the opposite of what was expected at this point and charge the human/rhinoceros hybrid instead.

Yeah, Michael wasn't up for that.

'Arrrrrgghhhh!' The sound of Michael's panic was loud enough to rise above that of the crowd, but only for a brief second because his leading toe caught the lip of a cobble, stopped his foot dead and pitched him off balance. His arms cartwheeled as he tried to stay on his feet, but knowing he was doomed if he didn't make it out of the alley and back into sight of the people in the cathedral plaza, made no difference to whether he did or not.

The ground came up to meet him as he sprawled across the cobbles and his breath rushed from his lungs in a painful whoosh of outrushing air. He had maybe two seconds to get moving again before the ghoul would be on top of him and that just wasn't enough. Heart pounding, he rolled over to face the horror bearing down on him and finally got a good look at the thing's face. It was a greyish white and the features were all out of proportion. Its chin seemed elongated and the nose was far larger than it needed to be to suit the face. The ears too were oversized, but Michael's attention was drawn to the hands which were already reaching down to grab him.

Trying to scramble back though he knew it to be hopeless, nothing could have shocked him more than the swish of something passing over his face and the ghoul's hands both jerking back to avoid it.

'Be gone, foul beast!' roared a voice Michael knew.

The ghoul had danced back a step, showing surprise and possibly confusion. Seeing it, Michael realised it hadn't really shown any expression on its face until that point. It was as if the thing wasn't connected to what it was doing or had no emotional connection to the horrible acts it performed.

There was no time to discuss such topics for the ghoul had recovered from its initial shock and was coming for him again.

Frank, the owner of the voice, stepped over Michael, hefting a double headed axe. It looked to weigh as much as the bookshop owner, but it was enough to make the creature question what it ought to do next.

'I said begone!' Frank shouted again, perhaps using volume to augment his threat and make him seem braver than he was feeling. Another probing swing drove the ghoul back a foot, but Frank was not well balanced with his weapon and the inertia of the axe made him pivot dangerously around and away from the ghoul as he tried to slow its motion. If the ghoul were to catch the axe shaft, it could kill them both in seconds.

Mercifully, a horn sounded at the other end of the alley and that caught the ghoul's attention. It turned and ran, heading away from them and down the tight alley to a silver van at the other end.

The sound of a police siren seemed to spook whoever was in the van though because it took off, burning rubber before the ghoul could get to it.

Galvanised into action, even though he was shocked to be alive, Michael pushed down the pain in his ribs and shoved himself off the ground. The ghoul was on the run, and it looked like its ride just left him behind.

Frank was still holding the axe but looking like it was

getting to be too much effort already. It wasn't so much that Michael wanted to chase the enormous creature, more that he never thought to question whether he should.

Snatching the axe from Frank, he yelled, 'Come on, Frank! We've got it on the run!'

Look Out! He's Got an Axe!

SATURDAY, DECEMBER 24TH 1737HRS

Yelling a battle cry, Michael charged down the alley, getting his feet up to speed just as the ghoul reached the High Street and turned left. The van had gone right, so he wasn't trying to follow it, but where was he hoping to go?

The double headed axe had to weigh at least fifty pounds. Goodness knows what size of man it was originally made for, but it would exhaust anyone in battle in seconds and was having that effect on Michael Michaels right now even though all he was doing was carrying it.

There were sirens in the air, the police converging on their general location, Michael prayed. Now was not the time to throttle back and let them take over the chase though, the quarry was running and even though he had no plan to swing the axe or cause harm, he hoped its presence might give the ghoul reason to pause until the police could catch up.

From the High Street, the screams of terror he expected to hear were strangely absent, but he saw why the moment he reached the end of the alley: to his left, the parade of ancient shops were undergoing construction work, their front façades covered in both scaffold and hoarding. The ghoul was running through the tunnel it formed and was hidden from sight. The pedestrians in the High Street elected to stay in the middle of the cobbled road rather than venture into the dark tunnel which gave the ghoul a safe route of escape. Following would leave Michael in an enclosed space with the huge creature and simultaneously give him no room to swing the axe, the only thing that might even the score a little.

On the ground was the creature's top hat – it had fallen off as he ran. Without thinking why, Michael scooped it as he started running again, stuffing it onto his head to leave his hands free.

A shout came from behind, but it hadn't come from Frank who had caught up already. Pumped on adrenalin, when Frank appeared at his side holding a pair of wicked curved knives, Michael put his head down and pushed his pace. His body, especially his joints, would demand payment later, but for now it answered the rally cry. Going around the hoarding, Michael almost ran straight into a couple pushing a baby in a stroller.

Screams lit the air as the mother reacted in shock. She wasn't alone though as her scream made everyone else look her way. What they saw was two crazy men running down the street holding weapons.

Michael hurried on, trying to track the ghoul as it ran through the hoarding. Judging the echoes, it was ahead of them, but they were catching it. Ten yards in front, the giant thing burst back into sight as it reached the end of the covered walkway, but by then it was almost at the end of the High Street and was coming into the open. Everyone would see it now and there would be no way for the ghoul to outrun the police when they arrived.

The sirens were drawing closer, giving Michael reassurance that this would be done soon but also convincing him to push harder now to close the distance and corner the ghoul. He hadn't run like this in years and was feeling it everywhere as his body demanded he stop.

The ghoul reached the end of the High Street and ran straight across the junction leading from the esplanade onto the bridge. Horns blasted as cars screeched to a stop and pedestrians on the bridge screamed at the horror headed their way. But the ghoul didn't go for the bridge, he went left, straight for the wall bordering the river. There, right in front of Michael's disbelieving eyes, the ghoul leapt the wall in a single bound and vanished into the blackness beyond.

Though he stumbled slightly in his surprise, Michael carried on until he reached the wall. He and Frank both heard the splash before they got there, slamming into the ancient stone to peer over the top of the five-foot-high structure. Light reflecting from the bridge allowed them to see where the ghoul had entered the water but there was no sign that it had surfaced.

'Put the weapons down!'

The loud voice came from behind, pulling their focus away from the water where they discovered half a dozen cops now staring at them. They were not armed with anything other than batons, but most likely had an armed squad of reinforcements inbound to their location. Michael realised it was their shouts he heard when he and Frank left the alley and the officers had been chasing him ever since. Had they even seen the ghoul?

Michael opened his mouth to say he would of course put his weapon down now the danger had passed, but no sooner did he open his mouth than another of the cops spoke. 'My lord, it's him again. And this time he's got an axe.'

It was Gaz, the cop from earlier who got so excited about the pocketknife Michael always carried.

'What about the ghoul?' Michael asked. 'You saw us chasing it right?'

Gaz had his cuffs out already. 'I saw two crazy men scaring people with weapons. That's affray at the very minimum.'

Frank spun the knives so they were pointing blade in and lowered them to the street. Michael crouched also, feeling a twinge in his back as he tried to get up again. They both had their hands raised as the cops moved in and now that he had time to gather himself and look around, he saw the sea of terrified faces all looking his way as if he were the source of danger.

Just before the police officers reached them, Michael asked Frank a question, 'This ever happen to you before?'

Frank nodded, looking bored. 'Yes. This is where we get arrested.'

Waste of an Evening

SATURDAY, DECEMBER 24TH 2157HRS

When they came to get him from his cell, Michael Michaels was surprised at how little time had passed. A monosyllabic constable in uniform let him out. The man was in his late thirties and doughy around his middle. He was efficient though, and perhaps the lack of conversation was part of the job.

The officer led Michael to an interview room where two more officers were waiting. He recognised neither but they stood as he came in and introduced themselves as sergeants Musgrove and Williams. He was invited to sit, and they went through the preliminaries of setting up the interview for the sake of the recording equipment.

Michael waited, somewhat impatiently for them to finish, then went on the offensive. 'Am I to be charged with something?' he demanded to know.

'You certainly could be,' answered Sergeant Williams, a stern-looking man with his grey hair parted to the left side of his head. He had steel-blue eyes that imparted an unspoken threat, and they didn't blink as he tried to stare Michael Michaels down.

'That's a no then, isn't it,' Michael concluded. 'I interrupted what looked like a kidnapping and gave chase. You've already confirmed the latter part of that from eyewitnesses though, haven't you? Why don't we skip to the end of this and you let me out with a warning to not run through the streets with an axe. Then I can get back to my wife and salvage what is left of Christmas Eve. How does that sound?'

As if ignoring that Michael had spoken, Sergeant Williams gave him a piercing stare and asked, 'Where did you get the axe?'

Michael certainly wasn't going to point the finger at Frank. 'It was to hand,' he replied.

Still refusing to blink, Sergeant Williams growled, 'I could charge you with affray.'

'But you already decided not to because you believe that I was a well-intentioned bystander who ran to the aid of a person in trouble. Did you catch the man in the van, by the way?'

Sergeant Musgrove shot his partner a look and sat forward in his chair. Speaking for the first time, he asked, 'What van?'

Michael threw his arms in the air. 'The silver van the man was driving. The ... thing I chased ...'

Williams interrupted him with a snort of laughter and smiled broadly. 'Ah, yes, the ghoul. Isn't that what you called it?'

'You can call it what you will. It is over seven feet tall and looks dead. When I saw it in the alleyway, it had a man by the throat and when I got close, another man appeared from the shadows. He was dressed in the clothes of Charles

Dickens which were stolen from the Dickens Museum three nights ago.'

'Wait.' Williams held up his hand to stop Michael speaking. 'You saw a man dressed as Charles Dickens?'

'Yes.'

'In the vicinity of the Dickens stage production in the castle?'

'Yes.' *Where was he going with this?*

Williams looked at his partner. 'Isn't it traditional for people attending to dress up for the occasion?'

Musgrove nodded. 'Many do.'

'So what?' Michael demanded. 'What are you trying to say? That all I saw was a man dressed up for the night and I imagined the rest? That the man I saw getting strangled was part of a street theatre act?' He thumped the table with a frustrated fist, drawing a warning look from both men opposite. 'The man in Charles Dickens clothes took the victim to a silver van and escaped the scene. I think the ghoul,' he said *the ghoul* with added emphasis and ignored that Sergeant Williams grinned again and mugged away to his partner, 'was supposed to get into the van too.'

'Did you get the van's registration number?' asked Musgrove, taking this more seriously than his colleague.

Michael made an annoyed face. 'I didn't get the chance.'

'Why not?' Williams wanted to know.

'Because I was too busy chasing the ghoul,' Michael snapped, his impatience making its way to the surface.

'Yes,' agreed Sergeant Williams, 'along Rochester High Street on Christmas Eve, among hundreds of pedestrians with a double-headed axe held above your head.'

'Did you see the body being loaded into the van?' Musgrove asked.

The Ghoul of Christmas Past

Michael opened his mouth to answer, but knew that if he said yes, he would be lying. 'No,' he admitted.

Musgrove pressed him, 'But you did see the driver and it was this Charles Dickens character?'

Again, Michael had to admit that he hadn't actually seen the driver. He had assumed, because of the circumstances he witnessed, that the third man in the alley took the van and put the victim in it.

The interview went on like that for another fifteen minutes. They believed the story about the ghoul, but they were not doing anything about it. No one was reported as missing. No one else had seen the attack, not even Frank. According to Musgrove and Williams, Frank heard Michael shout something and go into the alley. Frank saw the ghoul but didn't see the other man or his victim and no one else had seen the van. It was only because the police could corroborate Michael's story about the giant figure crossing in front of cars by the river that caused them to let him go with a caution.

He had to go through the process of having his personal effects returned, among which was his phone. The battery was in the red but would hold on long enough for him to call Mary – a task he did not currently relish. Unsurprisingly, he had a stack of missed calls and some strongly worded text messages.

He was looking down at his phone when the officer placed a broken top hat on the counter. 'That's not mine,' Michael said, wondering why he'd picked it up in the first place.

The officer shot him a look. 'You came in with it, therefore it's yours. This isn't a lost and found storage facility.'

Michael almost asked where he could find the nearest trash receptacle but spotted something poking from the black band going around the hat. It was nothing more than the top corner of a ripped piece of card, but his eyes immediately identified it. He hadn't seen one like it in years.

He signed for the items, said thank you, and confirmed he was free to go. However, he only went as far as a line of plastic chairs where he sat to inspect his find. Using a thumbnail to hook an edge, he pulled the ticket stub free. It was a dull purple colour with black ink, just like they used to dispense in cinemas and clubs when he was much younger. A person handed over their coins and the person in the booth hit a hidden button somewhere behind the counter causing tickets to shoot from a tiny slot in the steel surface.

That's what it was, but its nature was far less interesting than where it was from.

Frank was waiting for him outside. 'I was starting to think they weren't going to let you out,' he said by way of greeting, nudging himself upright from a position slouched against the wall. 'Poison is waiting around the corner with a van.'

Michael nodded. 'Good.' He held up the ticket stub so Frank could see it.

'Dickens Greatest Works Theme Park?'

'That's the part that has been missing,' Michael announced. 'All this time, I thought this was to do with the museum but that's not the case. At least, I don't think it is. The curator there is up to something; I haven't worked out what that is yet. I don't think it's connected to the ghoul though. I think the two things are separate and that is what has been throwing me.'

Frank asked, 'We're still going after the ghoul, right?'

Michael snorted a laugh of hopelessness. 'Surely, you have to be kidding? I thought that thing was going to kill me earlier. I don't know what came over me when I decided to chase it, but I won't be doing that again in a hurry.'

'What then?' Frank wanted to know. 'You said it took someone earlier. Did the police believe you? Are they going to deal with it?' Michael puffed out his cheeks – they both knew the police were not committing officers to investigate the possibility of a ghoul. 'Then we have to do it,' Frank concluded.

Michael did not like that plan. 'If I get killed on Christmas Eve, Mary will kill me.'

Frank tried to work that scenario out in his head but had to give up after a few seconds. He shook his head to clear it. Trying a different tactic, he said, 'Brother Grey Fox, ask yourself, what would Tempest and Big Ben do?'

Dammit. That was an unfair tactic.

Beginning to feel like there was no longer a way out of this, he argued, 'Big Ben would shag all the girls and knock the ghoul out with one punch while Tempest said something cool and got arrested. I can't do those things at my age.' Thinking about Big Ben's habits, he added, 'I'm not sure I ever could.'

'But you've already been arrested, Grey Fox,' Frank soothed, 'and so far as we know, there are no girls involved. Besides, all we have to do is go to the theme park and see if you are right. Once we get there, we can call the police and report what we have found.'

Michael knew Frank was right, but that wasn't going to make the phone call to Mary any easier. With a reluctant sigh, he placed the phone to his ear.

'Michael Michaels, I cannot believe you got yourself arrested!'

Perplexed by the mixed signals hitting his brains, Michael took the phone away from his ear to look at it. It hadn't connected yet. In fact, he could hear it ringing, but that meant … He looked up and saw the panic in Frank's eyes.

'She's behind me, isn't she,' Michael asked with a fearful gulp.

Frank backed away, nodding his head as he went but never taking his eyes from the approaching menace.

A few choice words, some rather colourful, bounced around in his head, then with a sharp sniff of the cold winter air, he spun around to greet his wife. 'Sweetie, how are you? You're looking so lovely this evening. How was the show? I'm so sorry I missed it, but I did get your chestnuts.' he pulled the packet from his pocket only to discover the paper they were in had lost its integrity and ripped.

Chestnuts spilled onto the pavement forcing him to hurriedly shove the bag back into his coat.

'Don't you sweet talk me, Michael Michaels,' Mary ground to a halt just inside trouser kicking range and wagged a finger at him.

Oh, no! She's using the wagging finger.

Mary couldn't hear her husband's thoughts, but she wasn't going to let him say another word. 'I had to sit through that whole performance alone and I was parched. I couldn't go to get my own drink because I would have lost my seat to someone else so I had to sit there thirsty for almost three hours.'

'That's what you are upset about?' Michael questioned.

Mary lifted her hands like she was going to throttle him. 'Arrgh! No, Michael. I am upset because I was worried about you. I had no idea where you had gotten to, though I assumed it was to do with your daft need to be adventurous like your son. I kept trying to call you and I was getting more and more worried and then I called the police and they said you had been arrested.'

Michael could see how upset and scared his wife was. He'd been ready for something of an argument, but he pulled her into him now, wrapping her up in a warm hug. Placing a kiss on the top of her head, he said, 'I saw a man being attacked. I had to go to try to help. Anyone would have done the same.'

'No, they wouldn't,' she argued.

He conceded that she was most likely right. 'But it is what I did. One thing led to another, Frank came to my aid, we gave chase and the police arrested us because the person we were chasing escaped.' He thought it best to say it was a person and leave the word 'ghoul' out. Using it hadn't done him much good so far.

Noises from behind him made Mary move her head to see what it was, and feeling his wife stiffen, Michael let her go so he could swing himself around to protect her if necessary.

He almost said, 'Holy Cow!' but managed to change it before the words left his lips, coming out instead as, 'Holy ... Good evening. This is Poison, yes?' he asked Frank and dipped his head at the small Chinese woman.

She shook her head. 'No, I'm Athena. This is Poison.' Coming out of the dark was another Chinese woman and she was flanked by two men, both also Chinese.

'Are you human?' asked Mary, unsure what she was looking at. She didn't believe in the supernatural, but the Bible didn't talk about aliens from outer space so maybe that's what they were.

The four young people looked at each other, mystified by the question. They each wore makeup, the guys included, and it gave them angular lines to their faces, accenting their cheekbones to make them look like they jutted out. The guys' hair was styled into spikes and one had frosted tips that glowed in the dark. Everyone wore black but each outfit was styled with a different colour that peeked through the tears in the fabric of the outer garments and above all, their clothing was tightly fitted to their bodies. Mary's assumption that they were from another planet was not without merit.

It was Athena who answered, 'Nah, we're in a band. I usually go by the stage name of Mistress Mushy.' She pointed to the two guys. 'This is Hatchett and Bob.'

'Bob?' Michael had to query it because against the backdrop of Poison, Mistress Mushy and Hatchett, it seemed a little bland.

Bob explained. 'It stands for Beyond Belief. Mum always said I was beyond belief. I guess I got into trouble with her a lot when I was little. It stuck and dad started calling me Bob. That stuck too.'

Frank clapped his hands together, breaking the moment. 'Right, that's the introductions done. Let's go get this ghoul then, shall we?'

Mary grabbed Michael's arm. 'Don't you move a muscle, Michael Michaels. You need to come home right this minute. You've gotten in enough trouble for one day already.'

'We're just going to take a look, love,' he assured her. 'It's important. The man I saw was hurt and they might mean to kill him. The police didn't believe me and all we want to do is see if we are right about where they have taken him. After that, I promise we will call the police.'

She shook her head vigorously. 'No. I heard the strange man who looks like a weasel,' Frank frowned at her comment, 'just say it is a ghoul you are after. I don't know what that is, but it does not sound like a church-sanctioned Christmas Eve activity. You're coming home.'

Michael pulled her into another hug. 'I can't, darling. I really wish I could, but I know someone is in trouble and police are not doing anything about it. I can't stand by and then read about their murder in the paper. I need to at least try.'

Mary wailed, 'This is a job for Tempest and that giant friend of his.'

His quiet reply stilled her arguments, 'He is not available, dear.'

Sneaking in the Dark

SATURDAY, DECEMBER 24TH 2218HRS

There was no chance Mary would go in the band's van to get there, so she followed in her Ford Escort. Michael sat in the passenger seat, watching to see if she would change her mind and just try to drive him home. Thankfully, she didn't, and they arrived at Chatham Docks, a largely abandoned former hub of industry and manufacture right on the river's edge. A few businesses were still operating but the area was dominated by the theme park which had now also failed and closed its doors for good.

They were close to the historic Royal Navy Dockyard where Michael worked occasional shifts as a tour guide. Michael knew the area well and knew a place to park where security patrolling the area would be unlikely to spot them. Not that security were the enemy; they might even be needed, but to get to the theme park, Michael, Frank, and everyone else would have to go unnoticed to begin with.

Getting out of the camper van next to them, Poison and her friends had all donned black masks that covered their heads. They looked like ninjas and to his disbelief, Michael watched them begin to unload weapons.

Frank held up a baseball bat with a grin. There was something written down the side of it. 'They wouldn't give me back my axe,' he said, as if that explained things. The ninjas were hefting an assortment of blunt weapons: a staff, nunchucks, a pair of sticks that Michael could not remember the name for.

'You should stay in the car,' Michael cautioned.

'You can get stuffed, Mr Michaels,' replied his wife, leaving little ambiguity regarding her thoughts on the matter.

Holding up his hands in supplication, he backed away from the car. 'I was just thinking about your safety and comfort, dear.'

'Knickers. I've got to come with you to make sure you consider your own safety. Without me there to stop you, you might try scaling the wall to follow Weasel Man and the Freak Show.'

Michael sighed. 'Can you just call them by their names, love?'

Mary argued, 'They're too hard to remember.'

Her reply got a raised eyebrow. 'Really. I doubt I could forget their names if I lived to be a thousand.' Letting the subject die and praying his wife wouldn't cause him too much embarrassment, Michael caught up to the others as they sidled to the corner of the old industrial park. The first building was a long-forgotten factory but peering around the corner, they could all see the front façade of the theme park.

One thing was clear: It was closed. Like forever.

'It does not look like there is anything going on in there,' commented Michael, holding up his ticket stub and wondering if he'd bought a red herring.

'Oh, well,' said Mary. 'Can't be helped. Let's get back for a drink before bedtime.'

She started to tug at his arm, but Michael slipped free. 'There's a cut through in the corner to get to the river. I bet we can access the back of the building from there.'

He started forward, Frank and his four black-clad ninjas sticking to the dark. In contrast Mary strolled out into the moonlit carpark area, refusing to play along.

'Darling, we have to stay hidden,' Michael urged, grabbing her arm to pull her back into the shadow. She muttered the whole way, making sure he could hear what she was saying by being loud enough that everyone could hear her, including any security guards who were not asleep in their cars and probably the bad guys if they were here.

It was a surprise then when they made it to the far edge of the factory unchallenged and found the cut through Michael claimed was there.

'How did you know about this?' asked Frank.

Michael shrugged. 'These buildings have been here since before I was a kid. I used to come down here with my friends to go fishing in the fifties. Some things change, but a lot of stuff stays the same.'

They all sloped along the space between the buildings, going around the puddles they could avoid and trying not to get too wet in the ones they couldn't. 'Michael, I have evening shoes on,' Mary pointed out, forcing him to go back and carry her across one that was deeper than an inch.

'Goodness,' he gasped under his breath as he picked her up.

Her eyes narrowed to slits as she glared at him. 'Got something to say, Michael?'

The Ghoul of Christmas Past

'No, dear. No nothing at all. I was just remarking to myself that I expected you to be heavier than that. You are as light as a feather,' he lied.

Her eyes did not relax. If anything, they narrowed even further. 'So you think I look heavy then?'

Accepting that he couldn't win no matter what he said, he placed his nearest and dearest back on the ground and carried on after the smaller shadows moving ahead of him. They reached the end of the buildings which terminated just twenty feet before the river. At the back, the dockside had no protective wall; a person could walk right off the side. It was more than a century old and intended for offloading. The river was high tonight, but the drop to the water from here was still fifty feet.

A ship-to-shore crane loomed overhead looking rusty, old, and long out of use. Its shadow came from the moon since there were no lights on anywhere in their vicinity. They had to watch their step, but as they rounded the back walls, intended to keep people out of the factory many, many years ago, they saw something that shouldn't be there.

A light in one of the back offices.

'Do you think that just got left on?' asked Hatchett.

Michael shook his head. 'I think there are people in there, and they are up to no good.'

'Then we should call the police,' insisted Mary, reaching for her phone.

Michael placed his hand over it. 'The light from that might draw their attention. All it would take is for someone to be looking this way, love. Anyway, there is no point calling the police yet: we don't have anything worthwhile to tell them.'

Frank nodded. 'He's right. They won't care that a light has been left on. At best they would send a squad car to the front entrance. They would get no answer and soon go elsewhere.'

'So what now then?' asked Mary, unhappy that they were not just going home.

Poison provided the answer. 'Hey, guys, I think I found a way in.'

Murder

SATURDAY, DECEMBER 24TH 2220HRS

The ghoul had squeezed Richard Glaagard's neck too hard, that was what it boiled down to. It was a simple mistake for the great brute to make but accepting his hurriedly revised plan hadn't been perfect hardly changed the intense frustration the man in the mask now felt staring down at the body. So much preparation, so much time and effort, and the man wouldn't get to see the truth because he was already dead.

'Put him with the others,' the ghoul's master barked.

The ghoul grunted a response, the best he could manage with his malformed mouth, and began to drag the lifeless form away by one ankle. Elizabeth Cudmore watched in abject horror, unable to speak or move much because she was bound and gagged. Richard was too, not that the effort was necessary in his case.

The message from James Pendergrass had troubled her, but it hadn't raised her suspicions. Looking back at it now, she couldn't believe how blindly she had wandered into the trap. Now she was going to pay for her lack of precaution with her life. It all seemed so unfair. And at Christmas too.

'Are you ready, Elizabeth?'

She shot tear-filled eyes at her captor, wanting to know why he was doing this but knowing she would not get an answer from the fifty times she had already asked. His misfortunes were not her fault. How could he blame her for them?

The man crouched next to her, touching her face with the back of his finger as if trying to smooth out a crease. 'You want to know why, don't you?' He nodded to his own question. 'You were so blind to what could have been, Elizabeth. All of you were, settling for recouping your investment instead of making a fortune alongside me. You just needed to take a risk.' Behind his mask, a smile tugged at the corners of his mouth, and he looked up and into the distance, focusing on something no one could see. 'There's a saying … you probably know it. "The biggest risk is taking no risk at all." Well that certainly proved true this time, didn't it? You played it safe and destroyed my work. MY WORK!' he thundered, making her cringe and flinch away. 'Selling to a bunch of real estate parasites. They'll tear this place down and build luxury apartments. Where is the grand vision in that? What will you have to be proud of and hand over to your children?'

She wanted to tell him it wasn't too late. That they could go back and reinvest their money now. But her words were coming out muffled through the gag and he made it clear he had no interest in hearing whatever lies she might try to spew.

The echo of heavy footsteps in the otherwise silent building soon revealed the ghoul. Richard's body was gone – "with the others" - Elizabeth remembered the instruction and it horrified her. Were *the others* the other shareholders? Were they already dead?

The Ghoul of Christmas Past

She couldn't ask, but her body wracked with sobs as the huge, white-faced ghoul lifted her from the floor.

Theme Park

SATURDAY, DECEMBER 24TH 2223HRS

Before anyone could respond, they heard machine noise from inside the building. Or rather, the noise seemed to come from beneath their feet. It eliminated any chance that there was no one inside, but the danger that the ghoul was in there got a whole lot more real suddenly.

What Poison had found was a set of stone steps leading down. They were carved into the inside face of the river wall and had to have been made when the wall was first built. They were slimy in places and the leading edge had been worn away from decades of use which made them treacherous. There was no handrail for support which made the going even tougher, except for Poison and her friends who bounced down the steps two or three at a time as if they were part of a parkour route. Frank adopted a more sedate pace though whether he did that to make Michael feel better, he didn't know and wasn't going to ask.

'What do you want to do, Mary?' Michael asked his wife. She wasn't dressed for exploring dark places.

She frowned at her husband. 'The same thing I have

wanted to do most of the day, Michael: go home. You're planning to go down there though, aren't you?'

He offered her a sad smile. 'Can you wait in the car? You can put the motor on. The moment I see something we can use to alert the police, I'll call you and let you know. You can call the police, and we can get out of here.'

Mary wanted to argue but helping those in need at Christmas was the right and Christian thing to do. It was also scary as hell and cold next to the water which meant waiting in the car was a much more appealing option. 'Just don't be long, Michael,' she pleaded with him. 'I worry about you.'

He was already two steps down but ran back up so he could hug his wife and kiss her. 'Get back to the car and stay warm. I won't be long.'

The concrete steps were worn smooth from years of use and slippery with a mix of water and dirt. It was even darker on the steps than it was on the jetty above but after only twenty or so steps - Michael hadn't thought to count – they levelled out to find themselves on a new platform.

Looking back up to the sky, Michael could see the old crane above them and nodded his head. Ships would have come alongside and the crane offloaded coal or whatever down into what must form a basement beneath what used to be a factory.

'It's too dark to go any farther, we'll need torches,' said Poison. 'There's all kinds of stuff on the ground. It looks like they just abandoned the place when it shut.'

Nodding back up to the light shining from a window above them, Michael said, 'It doesn't look like everyone abandoned the place.'

They pulled out their phones, lighting the low platform which revealed a silver van parked against a wall.

Wondering how on Earth they got it down here, Michael then spotted an access ramp on the other side beyond the van. It cemented any doubt they were in the right place. 'That's good enough,' he announced. 'That's the van I saw leaving Rochester High Street.' He might not have seen the man dressed as Charles Dickens loading the van or even driving it, but the coincidence was enough to convince him. 'We can call the police now.'

Michael bit the index finger of his glove to get it off and fished in his trouser pocket for his phone. It was down to almost no battery again, but there was enough to call Mary.

Except he had no signal. The concrete was blocking it. He swore but started toward the steps; he needed to go back up them anyway. When he noticed Frank and the ninjas were not following, he called out to them, 'What are you doing?'

Frank replied. 'We need to banish the ghoul, Michael. The police won't be able to deal with it. I thank you for getting us this far, but it's down to us to finish it now.'

'Are you crazy? It's just a really big man. Besides, we don't know that the ghoul is here. He went into the river. He might have drowned.'

'That which is already dead cannot drown,' Frank replied.

Michael shook his head with disbelief. 'Frank what we know is that the man who took whoever was in the alleyway is here. He was driving that van; I'm sure of it. That's kidnap and I'm willing to bet the victim was one of the shareholders. He took Ronald Norton three days ago, tried to get Richard Glaagard earlier this afternoon, and grabbed someone else this evening. I won't be surprised if he has the lot now, but it's a matter for the police.' His tone was insistent but had no effect on Frank.

'Call the police by all means, Michael. We'll have killed it, bound its soul, and left long before they show up. If we find any surviving humans, we will of course free them first, and if your Charles Dickens character makes an appearance, the police will find him tied up and ready for them.' That was his final word on the matter, for before Michael could say anything else, Frank pulled on his own black hood and they all extinguished their lights. The platform was plunged into total blackness, stunning Michael for a second, and when he swung the beam of light from his own phone across the concrete, there was no sign of them.

He cursed all the way back up the steps and along the cut between the buildings to bring him back to the front of the theme park. It was there that he found Mary's shoe.

Panic

SATURDAY, DECEMBER 24TH 2238HRS

His next few breaths came in desperate gasps as he tried to quell the wave of panic which threatened to drown him.

'Mary!' Michael spun around, rooted to the spot, and holding his wife's shoe. Yanking his phone out again, he stabbed the screen to rouse it, but nothing happened. The low charge had dropped to no charge, using it as a torch had drained the last of its juice to leave it nothing but a deadweight in his pocket. His eyes darted everywhere, searching for any sign of movement in the darkness and he bellowed her name again.

The sound of his voice echoed across the uncaring water and bounced off the empty buildings, but no answer came. His hands were shaking as his imagination delivered images and thoughts he couldn't bear to consider, and he ran. Splashing through shallow puddles he didn't notice his trousers getting wet and wouldn't have cared if he did. Mary ... his Mary, was missing and if she wasn't in the car, he didn't know what he would do.

He knew she wouldn't be, but he had to check anyway,

hoping with all his might that she would be in the car singing along to Cliff Richard songs on the music system. She wasn't though. He rounded the corner of the abandoned factory and could see how devoid of life the car was.

He ran to it anyway, performing the unnecessary check in case she was schooched down in her seat and asleep. Then he was running again, back to the theme park because that was where she had to be. The ghoul had her, and if not the ghoul then it was the Dickens wannabe.

The front entrance looked locked, but he checked it anyway, praying whoever grabbed Mary might have left it unlocked as they struggled with her. They hadn't. It was locked and solid; there was no way he could get in through it.

He was winded already, out of breath and doing his best to ignore his searing lungs and the pain coming from his knees and back. Gritting his teeth, he shoved away from the doors, propelling himself back up to something close to a sprint as he ran back around the side of the building and down the cut through to the river.

He was going to find Mary and he was going to get them both home and safe.

Mystery Guest

SATURDAY, DECEMBER 24TH 2246HRS

The ghoul dropped his latest captive into the seat next to Elizabeth Cudmore, the seat intended for Richard Glaagard. It balanced the boat and gave it a certain symmetry which the ghoul's master liked.

'Well done,' the man in the Dickens mask rewarded the ghoul with praise and got a happy, hopeful expression in return. Mary, scared out of her wits, saw the exchange, and tilted her head as she tried to analyse what she was seeing. 'Make sure she is secure but don't use the gag yet, I want to know who our mystery guest is.'

'No, you don't!' Mary snatched her hands away, but the ghoul grabbed her skull, one giant hand encompassing the whole thing.

'I wouldn't resist if I were you,' the man in the costume advised her. 'My ghoul accidentally killed Richard Glaagard when he grabbed him a few hours ago. He really doesn't know his own strength.'

Feeling like her head might pop, Mary chose to stop fighting but her mouth wasn't going to behave any more than it usually did. 'Who are you supposed to be then? Shakespeare?' she asked the man she could easily identify as Charles Dickens.

The man in the mask choked for a second and thought about having the ghoul snap the unpleasant woman's neck. His lips even twitched but he wanted to know who she was. 'You will tell me your name, or I will have the ghoul rip one of your arms off,' he snapped at her. He made it sound like it was a real threat, not just hyperbole.

Mary swallowed hard, gulping down the fear she felt as she considered lying or just refusing to give him the information he wanted. She tried a third option, asking him a question instead. 'How did you know I was outside?'

'Ghoul, take her left arm!' he was in the position of power and would not be defied by a pensioner.

Mary squealed and tried to duck away, yelling, 'Mary Michaels! My name is Mary Michaels, okay?' The ghoul was going to tear her arm off anyway. He'd had no instruction to stop. Feeling his massive hands tense in preparation to pull her arm from its sockets, she wailed.

'Stop.' The calm voice made the ghoul check over his shoulder and then step back. 'Mary Michaels. Wife of Michael Michaels I presume. I guess that means he is here somewhere also. Ghoul, find him.'

Breathing a deep sigh of relief, Mary watched the hulking man with the pasty white face lurch away, but he stopped when his master called to him. 'Ghoul. Kill him. Understood?' The ghoul nodded and rasped a word that could not be translated.

Once the ghoul was out of sight, the man in costume clapped his hands together, speaking inside his mask with an engaging, excited tone, 'I guess we are all here then. Perhaps we should get going before anyone else turns up and tries to ruin things. This took quite a bit of effort to arrange, so I hope you appreciate all the trouble I went to.'

He disappeared into a control booth, did something, and the boat started moving. It didn't go fast, the gentle current slowly tugging it forward and the ghoul's master was able to catch up and step into the front of the boat at walking pace.

Seeing that his latest captive, the one he didn't need, wasn't gagged he tutted and checked about his person. Finding nothing that would be of use he said, 'Mary I am going to be giving a presentation on this little ride. The persons seated around you are the shareholders who saw fit to withdraw their funding and send this theme park to the scrap heap. It is to be demolished soon to make way for new riverside housing, as if we need any more of that. Anyway, I must insist that you remain quiet throughout. I would ask you to save any questions until the end, but none of you will be able to talk when we get there. You see, the ride has a new finish to it, one where the floor actually gives way, and you cascade into the basement. It will be a bit like going over a waterfall only there's nothing beneath you but a terrible drop onto a hard concrete floor. I won't be with you for that bit. I'm the one shareholder who survives this tragedy.'

Blind

SATURDAY, DECEMBER 24TH 2253HRS

Michael Michaels didn't want to tread carefully or move cautiously. He wanted to run blindly into the old theme park, find Mary, and run out again. The problem he was currently having with that plan was the blind bit.

With no phone battery to give him torch function, he couldn't see a thing now he was back down at the platform outside the basement. He'd already hit his head on something made of steel that was jutting out just above his eyeline and cracked both his shins on a rusty old steel beam he hadn't spotted. That one had sent him sprawling onto the ground for what had to be the third or fourth time that day.

He had to hurry, but he couldn't, not if he wanted to avoid braining himself and regaining consciousness an hour later. Using his hands to sweep the air in front of his body and staying as low as he could, he stumbled forward.

He kept the pace up, believing that he didn't have far to go to the back wall of the building. There would be a door there, but how dark would it be inside? His old eyes did not see well in low light levels; it had stopped him driving at night years ago.

In the space between breaths, his retinas almost melted as floodlights above his head came on. Light came from inside the building too and he ran forward to a door now easy to see by the shaft of light coming around its frame.

It wasn't just light though, there was sound too, the sound of fighting. It had to be Frank and the ninjas. Had they found the ghoul? Or was it the Charles Dickens wannabe? Either way, when he spotted a loose piece of galvanised metal pipe lying on the ground, he snatched it up. It was three feet long and had a little heft to it. He smacked the free end into his left palm with a satisfying whack that made him feel a whole lot more confident.

Then he put his head down and started running again.

Presentation

SATURDAY, DECEMBER 24TH 2258HRS

'How did you know I was out there?' Mary asked less than a second after Charles Dickens instructed her to not speak.

He shot her a look and cracked his knuckles. 'I am beginning to tire of you, Mrs Michaels.' He'd been about to start the preamble for his presentation but only now that they were on the boat did he realised he'd never once thought to practice while moving. The boat went far slower than he'd allowed for and he needed to kill some time. 'Since you ask, it was your phone. You were making a call and it lit your head up to make it unmissable. It was luck also. You were right in line with the door when I returned to the flume ride with Mrs Cudmore. Had the timing been different, or had you been a few yards to either side when you made the call, I would not have seen you.'

Satisfied by his answer, she asked another. 'Why are you doing this?'

It was a very helpful prompt. A link, if you will, to the precise subject he wished to talk about. 'I'm glad you asked because it is time I explained.' He reached up and took off his mask and top hat, commenting, 'Goodness, it's quite hard to breathe inside those things.' He took a moment to wipe some sweat from his face with his sleeve, then proudly boasted, 'I'm Ronald Norton.'

'That's nice,' said Mary, being flippant because she had no idea who Ronald Norton was. But no sooner had she said it, than a voice in the back of her head told her she had heard the name before. She said it herself, 'Ronald Norton.' Then it came to her. 'You were kidnapped three days ago!'

Ronald Norton chuckled. 'Yes. Exactly right. That's what everyone knows. I was kidnapped by the ghoul. That is what they will discover anyway. The poor chap will have to die, of course, he has been a loyal servant. Incredibly loyal, truth be told. He obeys every instruction I give, no matter what I tell him to do. I'll have to test that later when I tell him to electrocute himself, but you wanted to know why, didn't you, and it is really quite simple.'

Battle

SATURDAY, DECEMBER 24TH 2259HRS

The sounds of mayhem were echoing through the structure as Michael made his way through the basement. He had no idea where Mary might be, only that she had to be in here somewhere. The building contained an entire theme park complete with rides and attractions which gave him a lot of territory to cover. Including the basement, there were three floors to search which was far too much. If he could find a landline, he would call the police, but until he did, or until he linked up with Frank and the ninja squad, he was going to have to do it all by himself.

With so much real estate to cover, some science or sense had to be applied, at least that is what Michael told himself. Trying to search every nook and cranny would take him days, and he doubted Mary had that long, so he was going to have to be clever.

She was taken at ground level, and the sounds of battle drifting on the air were coming from far away, so there was nothing happening anywhere near where he was. Most likely, the fighting did not involve Mary, unless Frank and the ninjas had come upon the ghoul and found her with him.

It had to be the ghoul too, Michael decided. Until now, he could have believed the ghoul drowned or was yet to make it back here after going in the river, but Charles Dickens would have lasted seconds against the ninjas. Michael could recall Tempest talking about tiny Poison fighting an army of clowns a while ago and how she wasn't to be underestimated. That meant they were fighting the ghoul and since the battle had been raging for half a minute already, they were not having an easy time of it.

Either way, if they had found the ghoul with Mary, she was probably going to be saved by them, but he needed to be sure. Breaking into a run again, Michael's pace was less than the sprint it had been but still fast enough to make him hurt. The source of the fighting was his destination, but in the otherwise silence of the basement, the sounds were bouncing between the equipment and echoing against giant storage tanks he could see lining one wall. Combined, he was trying to pinpoint a direction to head but having a hard time doing so.

After a full minute of running along passageways between machines and generators and other items of equipment he couldn't even identify, he was once again out of breath and wanting to slow. Frustration ruled his head and heart, but just as he wanted to scream at the sky, he rounded a ten-foot-high block of machinery and a cry of pain from either Poison or Mistress Mushy lit the air.

It was clearer than anything he heard before and gave him a distinct direction. Ten seconds later, he saw them. He wanted to increase his pace, but there was barely anything left in his tank now, pushing himself to keep going was the best he could do.

The Ghoul of Christmas Past

'Frank!' His yell when he saw the bookshop owner, caught the smaller man's attention. Frank had stepped into sight and then vanished again thirty yards ahead where the thin passage between machines opened out a little.

Cries of 'Waaaah! and 'Hatchaaaa!' were a constant from the four black clad fighters. They were giving all they had, but though Michael knew they were in the fight of their lives, he could focus only on finding Mary. His weary legs carried him to the end of the passage and there he got his first really good look at the ghoul.

Hatchett was lying against the side of a forklift truck, clearly in pain and without the weapons he came in with. Bob and Mistress Mushy were doing what they could to pin the ghoul back but could not risk getting close enough for him to grab them.

In the space of a second and a half, he saw Mistress Mushy swing a five-foot wooden staff in a twirl of precise movements which ended with a swipe at the creature's head. At the same time, Bob went in low with his nunchucks, aiming to fell the ghoul by taking out a leg.

The ghoul caught Mistress Mushy's staff with one giant hand, the sound like that of a baseball slamming into a catcher's mitt at high speed. His hand had to be almost the same size too. The blow to his right shin from a nunchuck moving at high speed made the ghoul roar, but otherwise had little effect as he tore the staff from Mistress Mushy's hands.

Now weaponless, the young woman flipped herself backward end over end to get away as the giant came after her. Bob tried to fell the giant again, drawing its attention, and then Poison appeared. She climbed onto a bank of machinery so she could attack from above.

They would win, Michael was confident, and they

would gain little if he pitched in to help them. Believing he was more likely to just get in the way, he grabbed Frank's shoulder, jolting the man who jumped at the sudden and unexpected presence.

Between laboured breaths, Michael shouted, 'Where's Mary?'

Frank's black hood was gone, and he had a nasty cut to the right side of his forehead Michael saw when the bookshop owner turned his way. Like Michael, Frank was gasping for air, effort and adrenalin placing demands on his body that would make anyone out of breath.

Frank sucked in a lungful of air so he could reply, 'Haven't seen her,' he gasped, opting for brevity. 'I thought she went back to the car?'

Grimacing at the news, which was both good and bad in many ways, Michael pushed on. 'They grabbed her,' he shot over his shoulder, certain that was the case even though she wasn't with the ghoul.

Michael did not want to abandon the team trying to contain and defeat the giant menace, but finding Mary had to take priority. There would be stairs to get him up to the next floor; he just had to find them.

The Big Reveal

SATURDAY, DECEMBER 24TH 2303HRS

'It was a dream of mine even when I was at business school,' explained Norton. 'I wanted to run a big business, to be the man in charge, but once I got there, I saw how small my dream was. I thought I would be the glorious leader, taking the firm by the hand to guide it into a new era of profitability, but I was wrong. I wasn't the leader. Oh, sure I got to make decisions on a daily basis, but the shareholders could veto them at any time, even when it made no sense to do so.'

The little boat meandered along the narrow river as he talked. His air was that of a tour guide though he wasn't saying anything about what they were seeing to the left and right. It was Mary's first visit to the park. Though she was a fan of Dickens, she was not a fan of theme parks in general and it had not once occurred to her to visit. Now, looking about, she suspected she had missed out. Inside the attraction, an entire story was being told, scene by scene, and the scenery and figures were incredible.

Norton continued to prattle on. 'Those three idiots

sitting in the boat with you ruined years of planning just because they got nervous. The park was close to losing money and what it required was fresh investment.' He made a fist and sneered as he claimed, 'We could have made this into Disney World. I invested the budget for new attractions into buying adjacent properties. The derelict buildings around us are all ours; the park could have grown in footprint by almost a thousand percent. Sure, there wouldn't be any profit for several years, maybe even a decade, but then what? Each of you damned fools would have been billionaires.'

Norton paused for a moment to check his position. 'Ah, here we are. Excuse me for just a moment, won't you?'

He got no response but wasn't expecting one. Mary watched him hop off the boat and jog forward a few paces to a projector set up behind a wall. As the boat drew level with him, he stepped back on and the projector came to life, shooting a picture onto a wall ahead of them. 'You'll have to excuse the crudity of my equipment. I was unable to secure the funds to buy all the things I needed. Apparently, banks do not give loans to people without jobs.' He said it with an angry growl, his remark aimed at the shareholders as they huddled, quivering in the boat.

Norton turned so he was facing away from them and looking at the images on the screen. 'Here you see the park as I envisaged it.' He continued to talk as the screen displayed a number of 3D images. Mary was no longer listening; she was trying to build up the courage to do what needed to be done. The ghoul was supposed to tie her bindings to a lashing point in the floor, one which had been added specially for this one trip; Norton didn't want his captives getting out. In his haste to obey Norton's command

The Ghoul of Christmas Past

to kill Michael, the lashing point was forgotten, and Mary had draped her skirt so it could not be seen.

She could rise from her seat and attack him, but her hands were tied behind her back so whatever she did, she would only get one shot at it. Nervously, she watched and waited.

The current carried the boat past the projected images and onward. Norton's voice was becoming a drone to Mary, and she was tuning it out. However, when he suddenly switched emotion and shouted at the people in the boat, she heard him.

He raged at them, 'You all ruined my plans for this place, and now I get to have my revenge by ruining your plans for life. You all thought you were cleverer than me, but that's not the case, is it? You'll all be dead soon; the plunge is right around the next bend.'

Behind their gags, the shareholders all whimpered and they thrashed against the bindings set into the base of the boat which made it rock. It made Mary feel a little queasy, which almost made her chuckle: getting seasick on a theme park ride. What would her husband, the former sailor, make of that?

'I had to rig explosives, of course. They'll go off before you get to them, so you know at that point that you've got only a few seconds left to live. I imagine it will be quite the ride though, just the sort of thing I would have added to the expanded park if you hadn't all been so blind.'

Norton, despite his outburst a few moments ago, was enjoying himself. It was almost done. Soon the shareholders would be dead, the interfering busybodies too and then he would have to kill the ghoul. His brow knitted. Where was the ghoul? Killing Michael Michaels should have been a moment's work. Why hadn't he returned? Inside the ride, he couldn't hear what might be occurring elsewhere in the building. Nor could he see what was beyond the inside of the attraction.

Feeling a little perplexed, and knowing that he was now short on time, he chose to reveal the biggest secret he'd ever kept.

'Do you want to know what happens to me after all this? After they get my call and come to rescue the one remaining survivor among the wreckage? Well, I'm glad I get to tell you because this is the best part. The dust will settle, but not before I get my face splashed all over the headlines: the tragic hero who killed a monster. It's not Kevin's fault – that's his name, Kevin – he was born like that. I found him on the internet. He worked at a circus in Blackpool where they used him as a strong man act. He's good like that. You tell him to pick something up and he'll do it. Even if it looks impossible to lift. Anyway, the bit these idiots in the boat don't know is that I caught the museum curator selling artefacts on the black market.'

His revelation made all three of the shareholders stop their struggling for a second. Even behind the gag, Mary was able to understand when Elizabeth asked, 'Really?'

Norton understood her too. 'Yes, really. I wondered if he had debt, or perhaps gambling issues or something, but I believe he is just greedy and thought he could get away with it. I went to him some time ago, hoping I could discuss with him the concept of moving the museum into the new theme park once we had expanded it. I needed to know what we could do together to make the museum experience better. He wouldn't discuss it. I mean ... he point blank refused to entertain the idea of discussing it, and he was cagey. So I sent him an email that infiltrated his system and cloned his hard drive. That sneaky git was selling rare first editions and other high value items to international bidders in an online auction room and then replacing them with cheap imitations. The museum visitors couldn't tell the difference, and all the displays are locked up and controlled by him. The perfect crime you might say.'

'Not perfect enough, clearly,' said Mary, causing him to look her way. There was a bridge coming up, one where visitors to the park could walk over and see inside the attraction. She had just seen something move up there and was very keen to stop Norton from seeing it.

Norton shot her a glare. 'I thought I told you not to speak.'

'Yes. Yes, you did. Sorry,' Mary apologised. 'It's just that you tell this story so well. I was feeling enraptured.'

Norton thought about screaming at her so she would stop interrupting but they really only had about a minute left before the turn and then the plunge. Plus, she had just given him a great link to the biggest piece of detail yet.

'Enraptured,' Norton repeated her word. 'It's funny you should say that because I will be using the brief fame of surviving the ghoul to launch my writing career. Tell me, how many novels did Dickens write?'

Mary didn't know the answer and could not make out what Elizabeth seated next to her was trying to say.

'The answer you want is fifteen,' Norton supplied. 'Only it's wrong.'

Around her gag, Elizabeth said, 'Really?' again.

Norton waggled his eyebrows. 'He had fifteen novels published, but he wrote twenty-two. Two of his unpublished works are complete and the other five are in varying stages of completion. When I turned the screw on Professor Loughborough, he was trying to find a buyer for the completed stories. No one in the world knows they exist.

Well, except for you lot, who will soon be dead, and Loughborough, who is already really rather dead. He was dumb enough to come here threatening me. Like the rest of you, he couldn't hold his nerves and see the risk through to the glorious end.

'So what are you going to do?' asked Mary, 'Reveal the unpublished works and become a hero of literature?'

Norton choked out a laugh. 'No, you silly woman. I'm going to rewrite them for the modern day and pass them off as my own. They are quite brilliant stories. Loughborough said he stumbled across them in a vault. They had been overlooked for over a century.' Whatever he might have wanted to say next was cut off as the boat passed under the bridge and a figure fell from it.

Final Battle

SATURDAY, DECEMBER 24TH 2309HRS

Michael arrived on the ground floor of the theme park out of breath and clinging to the bannister for support. The steel tube became a walking stick to help him along until he could get his breath back. The chance for that never came because in the silent park, the only noise was the steady thrum of machinery coming from one attraction.

The sound led him onward, his route easier to navigate now than in the basement because the passageways were clear and signposted. He hadn't gone far when he heard what sounded like someone speaking and that led him to a sign which claimed to be for access to the pedestrian upper gallery. It pointed into a narrow corridor which sloped up.

Michael took a moment to confirm the sound of the voice was coming from the corridor, and then he heard Mary. Clear as day, it was her voice, and his heart rejoiced. It also propelled him into the corridor but though he wanted to rush and leap out on whoever had her, he applied caution and took his time.

The corridor was dimly lit and wound around to the right.

As he followed the curve, light appeared ahead and the man's voice he heard first became clearer. He paused and held his breath for a second, listening to the voice. It was the same one from the alleyway: the man dressed as Charles Dickens.

This was it then. The ghoul was downstairs fighting a team of ninjas, so with luck it was now just Charles Dickens to face. All Michael had to do to win the day was defeat him, but as he peered around the edge of the corridor where it opened out onto what the signpost called the upper gallery, he saw it wasn't just Mary to rescue.

Mary spotted him and looked away, thinking of a question to draw the mad man's attention. He had been about to look forward in the direction of the boat's travel. Michael didn't think the man would spot him way up above his head, however, Michael got to see the man's face and all the confusion melted away.

He was looking down at Ronald Norton, the first of the shareholders to be kidnapped. Michael could find out why later, but it was clear he had to beat him to save everyone else and he had the element of surprise.

Michael waited until the boat passed beneath the bridge and then went over the side.

His timing wasn't perfect, and the blow Michael tried to land with the steel tube missed Norton's head, cracking him on the shoulder instead. It would still be a winning blow if he followed it up with another. Unfortunately, Michael's feet hit the unsteady deck, causing the boat to lurch violently. It threw him backward and off the tiny vessel.

Landing on the shore with a hard bump, everyone got to hear him swear about his hip.

'Ghoul!' Ronald screamed to the ceiling. His shoulder was a ball of pain, yet he rejoiced. He knew he would have to injure himself before the rescuers came to free him. No one would believe it if he came out of the tragedy unscathed. Now he felt like his shoulder was broken but the old man was down and easy pickings.

Michael wasn't going to be beaten so easily though. With a roar of defiance, he shoved the pain down and used the steel tube to help him back to his feet. The boat was continuing to move forcing him to limp after it.

'Hurry, Michael!' yelled Mary. 'He's going to blow out the floor and send us all into the basement!' The shareholders were once again struggling against their bindings and gags, sensing that this might be their last chance for salvation. Mary saw Ronald wavering on the bow and tensed her muscles. She could charge at him with her head and knock him from the boat. That might help Michael, but she would then have to work out a way to save the others without using her hands.

Seeing the old man get to his feet, Ronald stepped from the boat. He was going to have to do this himself.

Mary cursed herself for hesitating for in the moment she made the decision to rise and charge at Ronald, he stepped onto the shore.

Now facing his opponent, Michael had to choose between using the steel tube to support his gimpy leg or manage on one leg and wield it as a weapon.

Then he saw a third option.

Ronald took a pace forward; he was going to kick the old man's legs out and throw him into the river, when the explosion created a hole beneath the ride, a million gallons of water would flow out in seconds, carrying the old fool with it. However, Norton had no time to lose because the boat was about to draw level with the detonator. If he missed the timing, they would have to go all the way around again.

Michael limped two paces to a mannequin and there he plucked the sword from its hand. Now, with a mad expression on his face, he had the steel tube in his left hand to keep himself upright and a sword in his right. Ronald Norton could surrender or get skewered; it really would be his choice.

Ronald disagreed though, a smile spreading across his face as he looked beyond Michael and stepped back onto the boat.

Gripped by a sinking feeling, Michael spun around to find the ghoul bearing down on him. Most of its makeup was gone. The same thick white paste Michael found on his coat was what had been used to make the giant man look so ghoulish. It must have transferred to his coat when he was pushing through the bushes outside Richard Glaagard's home. However, working that part out did nothing to change that Michael was about to die.

Weary, in pain, and feeling exhausted, Michael figured he had just one chance to win now, and it would take perfect timing and the acceptance that he was going to have to suffer. He let the ghoul come, keeping his hands down and looking beaten – which wasn't a stretch.

The ghoul didn't have an angry leer on its face. It didn't really display any emotion at all as it reached for Michael, but as the hands came to grab his head, Michael waited until the ghoul was right on top of him, then he let the steel tube go. He fell backward, raising the sword as he went.

In the boat, Ronald Norton was back in charge. This was his great moment. He got to watch the shareholders die, and with them any chance of resurrecting his dream for the theme park. But from the ashes of his fantasy would spring forth a new dream, one where he didn't have to suffer such fools. He would become a literary sensation. He smiled at the helpless captives in the boat and slammed his hand on the detonator button as the boat drew level with it.

An almighty roar filled the air as out of sight around the next corner, the floor beneath the flume ride exploded. There was no smoke or flame, but the whole building shook and the air filled with vapourised water. The boat bucked as a wave pushed out by the energy of the explosion shunted them back several feet and Mary rose from her seat with her head down. Like a bull, she charged forward, her head her only weapon.

The ghoul had committed its bodyweight into the swing to grab Michael and finding nothing there, it overbalanced just as Michael expected. He was falling to the deck, bringing the sword around so it would jut upward like a spike the ghoul could not hope to avoid. Pain from Michael's hip when he hit the floor made him grunt but he held the sword and watched as the ghoul fell on to it.

The tip dug into the ghoul's chest right below his heart. It was a deathblow. Or it might have been if the cheap prop sword hadn't snapped off at the handle the instant it was required to do some work.

The ghoul landed on top of Michael with a thud, shunting all the air from Michael's lungs and making him feel like a sandwich on a panini press. That was when the shockwave from the explosion hit them. It seemed to terrify the ghoul who rolled to his side and away from Michael. A splash told Michael the ghoul was in the river, but if there were any advantage in that, Michael no longer possessed the physical ability to leverage it.

The wave that lifted the boat was almost instantly sucked back as millions of gallons began to pour through the ruined floor. The boat surged forward but Ronald expected all these things to happen and was mentally prepared for them. It was his decision to be up close so he could see the look in their eyes when the shareholders went to their deaths. All he had to do was step from the boat onto the shore and perhaps tip them a little wave as the outrushing water sped them to a painful, terrifying death.

What he hadn't planned for was one of the captives rising from her seat. He saw the grey-haired woman as she came forward but there was no time for him to react. No sooner had he cottoned on to what she planned to do than it was happening.

The crown of Mary's skull connected with Ronald's midriff just below his ribs. It winded him slightly, but more importantly it drove him from the boat. Arms spinning wildly in the air despite the pain coming from his ruined shoulder, he fell backward over the bow of the boat.

With her arms pinned behind her back, Mary was unable to stop her own forward motion and would have pitched out of the boat too had it not surged forward at that moment. Coming to rest half in and half hanging out of the boat, she got to see as Ronald tried to surface only to have the boat roll over the top of him.

Behind Mary, the shareholders were screaming inside their gags and now frantically trying to rip their arms from their own sockets if it meant they could just get free before the boat plunged through the hole they could not yet see.

Then the boat stopped. It jammed and held tight for a second and only Mary knew why. She was staring down into the water at Ronald Norton's face. It was contorted in pain and rage, but the ride had been designed to give only the minimum amount of clearance between the boat's hull and the riverbed and Ronald was now a wedge beneath it. His own body was preventing the boat from following the water to the hole.

On the bank, Michael rolled to his side. The ghoul might be wet, but it wasn't hurt, and Michael got to watch as it clambered back to its feet. Like Godzilla rising from the depths, water cascaded from his hair and clothing and once again he turned his attention to the man on the floor.

His last command had been to kill Michael Michaels.

Feeling like it might be simpler to just put his head back and accept his fate, Michael nevertheless pushed himself back and looked about for the steel tube.

Never give up.

The voice of his son, Tempest, resounded in his head. He might not stand a chance, but he would go out fighting.

'Kevin.'

The ghoul turned his head.

Mary was sitting on the bow of the boat, her hands still bound awkwardly behind her back. 'Hello, Kevin. That is your name, isn't it?'

No one ever called him Kevin. He looked back at the man on the shore remembering he had a task to perform and took a step forward.

'Kevin,' Mary called, getting his attention again. 'It's Christmas in a few hours. Do you like Christmas?'

This time the ghoul tried to smile. The effect was horrific, but Mary could see what it was trying to do. 'How about if we sing a Christmas song?'

Michael had no idea what his wife was doing, or how she knew to do it, but like a snake charmer lulling a serpent into a drowsy, compliant state, when she started singing Cliff Richard's biggest Christmas number one, *Mistletoe and Wine*, the ghoul dropped his menacing hands back to his sides and began to hum along.

The water in the artificial river was flowing around the ghoul's legs, the level getting lower by the second as it flooded the basement below. In a jolt of panic, Michael remembered Frank and the ninjas. They were down there still? That they were not here meant the ghoul had beaten them. What shape were they in? Where were they in relation to the hole that just got made or the water pouring through it? Had they been buried under tons of falling masonry, or drowned by the flood?

Michael was in no shape to help them, but Mary's singing shut off abruptly when the boat shifted. Mary almost fell overboard, something that would ensure her doom, and only stayed on the boat because she managed to hook a foot around the bottom of a seat.

Ronald was getting up and there was still enough water left in the river to carry the boat to its doom. With a triumphant roar, Ronald burst from the water, gasping for breath but leaping to the shore to clear the boat's path to the hole.

'Kevin!' Mary screamed. 'Help us!'

A beat passed as the ghoul stared at his master and back at the boat. Then he started wading, running through the water after the boat as it began to pick up speed.

Seeing him, Ronald shouted, 'Ghoul, no!'

The ghoul faltered, his steps slowing as conflicting instructions ruled his head. Mary's terrified wail, 'Kevin, save us!' broke the spell.

Just as the boat reached the corner, a giant hand grabbed the back end. It was three yards from the hole and the passengers could see the wreckage fifty feet below. If the ghoul let go, they would have two or maybe three seconds before the boat impacted on the floor below where it would explode into pieces.

The Ghoul of Christmas Past

Ronald couldn't believe what he was seeing. The ghoul was his servant! His to command! 'I said, no!' Ronald roared, jumping down into the last of the outrushing water. In a few more seconds there wouldn't be enough river left to carry them through the hole. He would not let this happen!

Charles Dickens fancy walking cane rose into the air and fetched down on the ghoul's shoulders with a terrible crunch. The ghoul cried out in pain but maintained his grip on the boat. Another blow landed, but as Ronald raised the cane to land another, it was plucked from his grip.

He spun around to find four battered looking ninjas staring back at him. The nearest of them, clearly a girl, said, 'I guess you're the dick in Dickens.' Then she kicked him in the nuts and punched his throat as he sagged.

Michael thumped the floor with an annoyed fist – he'd been waiting for a chance to deliver a killer line all day and Poison had just done it.

No one said anything for a second; they were all too terrified, emotionally exhausted, or just plain gagged to find any words. Then the hull of the boat hit the bed of the river and wedged there.

The ninjas were looking at the ghoul who was once again confused about what he was supposed to do. He didn't want to hurt people, but as a child he'd been taught to do as his elders and betters told him. He was too big, too dangerous, and too dumb to think for himself, so he'd always done as mummy said and when mummy was no longer there, someone else always came along to give him instructions.

Now he faced people who wanted to harm him, and he wasn't going to let that happen. Rounding on them, he raised his fists again.

'Kevin,' Mary called. Getting his attention, she then

addressed the ninjas, 'Take off your masks and smile at him. He's quite friendly really.'

Frank gave her an incredulous look. 'He's killed a whole bunch of people.'

Mary kept her smile and flared her eyes at him as Kevin looked their way again with menace in his eyes. 'He was just doing what he was told.'

Frank and everyone else started smiling like crazy fools, big grins plastered to their faces. Kevin tried to copy them.

'Now put down your weapons,' Mary instructed.

Ronald gave a groan and tried to get up. Kevin glanced down at the man who had been his master, made a decision, and punched him in the head.

Breathing a sigh of relief that it was finally over, Mary called to her husband, 'Michael dear, do you happen to have your pocketknife to hand?'

Aftermath

SATURDAY, DECEMBER 24TH 2323HRS

The police arrived a few minutes later just as everyone was trudging back out through the entrance of the flume ride. The ghoul was carrying Ronald, who was alive, but quite unconscious and Mary found her handbag. She took the phone from it, intending to complete the call that got cut off earlier when the ghoul grabbed her. She put it away again when she saw there was no need.

Flashlights shining in through the doors at the front of the theme park revealed the police standing just outside, but it was just the occupants of a single patrol car.

With no key to open it, Poison and Mistress Mushy had to find a fire axe to smash the doors.

'Is this it?' asked Mary. 'This is all they sent? I told them we needed the cavalry and to make sure they sent Chief Inspector Quinn.' She knew the name because Tempest was always saying it.

The two police officers were Dodds and Beaton, two female cops who would much rather be doing anything else on Christmas Eve than responding to calls. Dodds, a short woman in her early twenties with a boyfriend who was most likely right now out on the prowl for drunk, lonely women, said, 'There's another incident. Lots of the cops went there. What's been going on here anyway? Dispatch said there was a call for help that got cut off halfway through. The only thing they got was the location so asked us to do a drive by.'

Mary sighed and accepted that she was probably lucky the police turned up at all.

Michael, hanging between Bob and Hatchett who were battered and bruised but in better shape than the pensioner, asked, 'Is that when they grabbed you?'

Mary nodded and a smile flitted across her face that needed to be explained. 'Ronald said he wouldn't have caught me outside if I hadn't been making a call. It never occurred to him to ask who I had been calling.'

To the cops, Frank said, 'We've been through the wringer tonight, a couple of ambulances wouldn't go amiss. Also, we have three kidnap victims here and there are several bodies downstairs.'

'Bodies?' echoed Dodds.

Beaton had a different question. 'Who's been kidnapped?'

Elizabeth stepped forward and began to explain. The two police officers listened with incredulous expressions and took Ronald Norton into custody when he came to a few moments later. He looked dazed and was most likely concussed – not that anyone cared. Once loaded into the back of the car, Dodds drew the short straw and went to look for the bodies while Beaton began checking people over. Ambulances and paramedics were on their way and phones were handed out so the shareholders could speak with their families.

The three kidnap victims would get to go home soon,

but they were in the middle of nowhere on Christmas Eve and not even a taxi driver would come to get them down here.

Michael tapped Bob's arm and asked to be put back down on the carpet. 'Does anyone have a phone that works?' he asked once the shareholders had all made their calls.

Frank rooted in a pocket, moving gingerly because he had so many body parts that hurt, but found the item and handed it over. 'Calling Tempest?'

Michael shook his head. 'Robert Whittaker. I have something he would like to know.' Mary had already regaled him with the story about the museum curator and the thefts. Ronald must have decided he wanted the Dickens outfit to add a touch to his master plan but hadn't counted on the security guard doing his job right for once. With a chuckle, Michael handed the phone back without making any calls.

'Change your mind?' asked Frank.

Michael shrugged. 'I don't remember the number. I can call him tomorrow. It will make his day, I expect.' He drew in a breath and let it go through his nose – something was still troubling him. 'Mary, how did you know … Kevin,' like everyone else, Michael was having trouble adjusting to the idea that the ghoul he'd just spent the whole day chasing was now one of the good guys. That his name was Kevin, as mundane a name as one might find, didn't help. The ghoul, or rather, Kevin, without instruction to do something, was just standing to one side doing nothing. 'How did you know he would do what you asked?'

Mary had taken it upon herself to look after the giant hulking lump of a man, positioning herself so she was closest to him like a mother might with a nervous child.

'There was a man like this in the street where I grew up. He was a teenager by the time I was old enough to play outside, and he suffered from gigantism, much like Kevin here. He wasn't as big as Kevin and they didn't have a name for the condition back then, but I guess people would say he was a little on the slow side. I knew he was harmless, but he was also bigger than anyone in the town and that made people cross the street to get away from him. His name was Matthew. As a little girl I didn't know I wasn't supposed to play with him and got a proper telling off from my mum when she found me. Matthew was helping me learn to ride my bike, running alongside it to keep me upright.'

Mary had a faraway, sad look to her eyes, remembering something that still pained her. 'The local boys discovered they could get Matthew to do things. He just didn't know any better and he always wanted to join in and to please people. One day they got him to steal things, and when the police came, he hurt one of them and he was taken away. I never saw him again. I suppose Kevin will have to go away too.'

Michael nodded his head, seeing no other possible option. 'For his own safety as well as that of everyone else.'

A polite cough interrupted them, and they turned to see it came from Elizabeth Cudmore. 'I believe there may be another option.' Her opinion got lots of raised eyebrows, but everyone kept quiet to hear what she had to say. 'He saved my life and I think I speak for the other shareholders,' - (James and Mason exchanged a glance that said they didn't agree with whatever Elizabeth was about to propose though neither vocalised their thoughts) - 'when I say that I believe we can find a safe facility for Kevin. Such things exist. My brother is a high-court judge and will be getting a call in the morning where I shall ask him to perform a

Christmas miracle. Essentially, Kevin will go to jail,' Elizabeth saw Mary's frown, 'but the sort of jail where they are not confined to cells and have arts and craft classes every day. For someone like Kevin, I believe it will be like a permanent vacation.

'That sounds much more like it,' said Mary. Turning to face Kevin she asked. 'Would you like to go to a home where you don't have to do what people tell you all day? You'll be looked after, and no one will bother you. How does that sound?'

Kevin did the thing with his face that was as close as he could get to a smile. It still looked horrific, but Mary was becoming familiar with his expressions. She took his hand in hers which was a lot like when a baby holds their parent's little finger; it gave both Kevin and Mary comfort.

Elizabeth concluded, 'My business partners and I will set up a trust fund.' She heard the rustle of clothing as Jason raised his hand. 'Yes, we will!' she snapped, causing him to lower it again. 'He will be cared for.'

She looked around the room at Frank and his ninjas, at Mary holding the giant's hand and Michael Michaels, half crippled and sitting on the floor. 'What about the rest of you? We owe you our lives. Why were you even involved? You're not the police.'

Michael let a grin crease his face. This was his chance. 'Well, kitten, sometimes the world needs a hero.'

In the next second, Mary's phone bounced off his head.

Afterword

Hello, Dear Reader,

I hope you enjoyed this story. It is short for a novel, but officially novel length at over forty thousand words. I intended it to be a short story, which would have been no greater than half this length, but as so often happens with me, once I fall into story-telling mode, I have few controls.

I first thought up the concept of a killer dressed up as Dickens more than a year ago. I created a file for it and wrote a few lines of notes, but it sat on the planner until randomly, a few weeks ago, I decided to write a Christmas story. I have so many tales to tell that I might never get them all down on paper and my desire to push onward with two of my more popular series led me to put the next Blue Moon book on the back burner. It was supposed to be *The Sandman* that I wrote next and I know people are waiting for it. I allude to it in this book and the events of that story will overlap this one which is why this adventure, originally planned for Tempest, had to be written with Michael and Mary, his parents in the lead roles. I rather enjoyed it, but I promise *The Sandman* is coming and will do my best to make it worth the wait.

Dickens spent most of his adult life in the area where I grew up and now live and is synonymous with the local towns. Rochester High Street is littered with pubs bearing plaques on the wall proclaiming that Charles Dickens used to frequent their ale house. Chances are the claim in each is true. The museum is in Rochester High Street much as I describe it, though the curator probably isn't selling first editions on the black market. Chances are, he's a decent chap.

The theme park is a real thing too though it is called Dickens World. I went there some years ago though I do not remember who with or what we did there. It closed several years ago and I must confess I do not know why. My assumption is that it simply could not draw enough visitors, which is a shame. It sits on the river just as I describe but to either side one will not find derelict buildings and abandoned factories, but a vibrant leisure and retail park with restaurants, shops, bars, and a cinema.

Using the development of prime real estate as a motive for murder occurs in this book and it is not the first time it has cropped up. In the *Phantom of Barker Mill*, there is a plan to demolish the mill and turn it into luxury riverside apartments not far from the fringes of the capital. In the course of my life, I have seen many riverside areas, which were once industrial hubs, suddenly razed to the ground for the land to become expensive properties. Some are on the river in Maidstone, my local city, where I describe Big Ben's penthouse apartment, but they are everywhere, and I could probably find a dozen locations being developed within a few miles of me today.

The Mystery Men bookshop is fictional, but the location

of the bookshop is not. It is not there any longer, but as a child there was a shop called Stargate One which specialised in fantasy and sci-fi books. It sat above another shop with a door leading to stairs which in turn led up to the shop itself. I don't remember much about it other than in the late seventies, when Star Wars was all the rage, I bought a book in there called *A Splinter of the Mind's Eye*. It was a Star Wars spin-off novel.

I'm going to leave it at that and let you get on with whatever else you have planned. I need to go back over the whole manuscript and fix all the holes I will have left in the story. You won't know what I am talking about because you get to read the version after I fixed them.

Take care.

Steve Higgs

Next in the Blue Moon Investigations Series

vinci-books.com/sandman

In their deadliest adventure yet, Tempest and friends must save their missing team member before it's too late.

Jane has been taken by a serial killer known only as the Sandman, Tempest and friends must find her before night falls. Why so soon? Because that is when he kills his victims, bringing them dreams as he sings them to sleep. They sift through Jane's notes and piece together clues and half-baked theories in a desperate scramble to find the man at the core of the mystery.

Turn the page for a free preview…

The Sandman: Chapter One

MISSING TEAM MEMBER

Friday, December 23rd 1517hrs

Tempest

Amanda and I were all but running as we left the ward. My clothes were on - having dressed in a world record time – but crazily dishevelled and my hair had to be sticking out at all angles because that was what it always did until I tamed it.

None of these things registered in my head as both Amanda and I started talking.

We were having two different conversations, and neither was with each other. I was on my phone to Big Ben. Amanda was on her phone to Hilary.

Two minutes earlier, Chief Inspector Quinn had left my hospital room after dropping a bombshell about Jane. Jane is the third detective at my firm, Blue Moon Investigations, and she was missing. He didn't say she was missing, that would be poor form for a police officer, a senior one to boot, unless he was already doing something about it, but what he did say was enough for me to believe she was in desperate trouble.

Chief Inspector Quinn revealed that Jane had music playing when her phone was answered but there was no one there to talk to. Anyone else would most likely think that was odd yet dismiss it. Amanda and I knew what it meant, and it sent ice through our veins.

The piece of music was *Mr Sandman* by *The Chordettes*, and it was the signature of a serial killer we had dubbed The Sandman. Jane stole one of his recent victims before he could kill her and got a threat through the mail only days later.

It read: *I'm going to sing you to sleep,* and it came with a copy of the record to remove any ambiguity about the sender's identity.

Ever since, Jane had been working on her caseload while never really taking her eye off her investigation into who the Sandman might be in real life. I had left her to get on with it, never really paying enough attention to how great a threat the psycho posed. There had been no further threats from him, and no messages or signs that Jane was being followed. We also had no client for the case and lots of paying work to keep us busy.

I was going to blame myself if anything happened to her, and since she was most likely the captive of a serial killer already, I had to accept that something already had.

Big Ben's sleepy voice reached my ear. 'Hey, normal sized man, what's happening?' Big Ben is an old buddy from the army. He's six feet seven inches of toned, lean muscle with a face that could sell aftershave. He never misses a chance to be a dick.

I cut through all his nonsense fast. 'Jane's been taken, Ben. It's the Sandman.'

I got a beat of silence before he said, 'Where do you need me?' The tone of his voice and entire attitude had switched in a heartbeat. We were dealing with serious business and he was ready.

He got the short answer. 'The office. Amanda is with me. We are just leaving the hospital to get to Rochester. We need to go over Jane's notes first. She's been trying to work out who this guy is for weeks. It's time to finish her work.'

'Okay.' I could hear movement in the background and a woman's voice. Strike that, I could hear at least two different voices – two women. At least. 'I need a few minutes to organise myself. I'll meet you there.'

With that call complete, I called the next number on my mental list. I have a circle of friends just like anyone else. Unlike most people, mine were all heroes. They chose to involve themselves in my work, coming with me when I needed extra muscle or extra brainpower. It rarely goes well.

I called Jagjit, a man who I met at school on my first day. Our careers diverged when we left school, he went to university and I went off to be a soldier. When I left the army and returned home, he was still there, and we picked up where we left off.

Amanda caught my arm to get my attention as the phone rang in my ear. We were still negotiating our way through the crowded hospital and I looked around expecting to see that she was trying to steer me away from something.

It wasn't that; Amanda had something to tell me and a question to ask. 'Hilary is on his way. His wife is not happy.' When was she ever? 'Do you want me to call your parents?'

My mum and dad are kind of kooky. Dad is retired

The Ghoul of Christmas Past

Royal Navy and is the kind of man who gives his son a stupid middle name because he believes it will help him in life. It didn't. Mum crosses herself thirty times a day, tipples on gin and wine and dreams up ways to annoy my father. She vehemently disapproves of my career as a paranormal investigator – my activities cause at least half of the crossing she does – while dad thinks my job is brilliant and keeps joining in.

He has nearly died while helping like eleven times already. He's probably the reason mum finds the need to tipple.

I pursed my lips and shook my head. I didn't want them dragged into this. It is only a day until Christmas, and they are heading to my sister's place in Hampshire for the big day. We would have enough people to go over the information I expected to find.

Having given Amanda my answer, I continued planning in my head. The exit was ahead but we had to slow down as we reached the press of people in the hospital's reception area.

Jagjit finally answered his phone. 'Tempest, what's up?'

Oh, yeah. I should probably introduce myself. My name is Tempest Michaels. I'm a six-foot, one-hundred-and-ninety-pound former British soldier and current paranormal detective. The current job came about by accident but has stuck because it seems to suit me. I employed Amanda because she asked me to, and I said yes because she is a drop-dead gorgeous blonde and the thing in my pants makes decisions for me all too often.

This story is about me. Kind of.

The Sandman: Chapter Two

UNPLEASANT SENSATION

Friday, December 23rd 1518hrs

Jane

I awoke with a dry mouth. That was the first thing my brain chose to notice, but it took no more than a heartbeat for it to catch up with some of the more pertinent information. Such as my hands being tied behind my back. A ball of cotton wool filled my mouth, hence the dryness, and the moment I felt it there I began to gag. It was held in place by a rag which was tied tightly around my head.

Forcing myself to calm, I got the gagging under control and ran a mental checklist to see what other problems I might have. I couldn't see anything, but I wasn't blind, I was simply in a room devoid of light. I was lying on a bed. A comfortable bed at that; not that being comfortable was giving me any comfort.

Doing my best to think logically, I worked back through

recent events. I'd just arrived home late last night, only leaving Frank's super-creepy house in the countryside once I knew Tempest, Amanda and the others were safe. They'd been tracking a team of ex-special forces guys and it all got a bit tense for a while.

They lost Tempest in the woods and couldn't get hold of him. I stayed with Frank until we heard he'd been found, cold, but unharmed.

So I left Frank's house, driving my car back to Gran's house in Aylesford ... but then what? I had a vague sense of arriving home. Exhausted, starving, and wanting a bath even though it was something like two in the morning, I ...

What did I do? I asked myself the question as I wriggled around and tested my bindings. My ankles were tied too, but not my knees which meant I could shuffle my legs around. The ropes – it felt like rope – around my ankles were tight but had been tied over my boots. I was going to be able to get my feet free if I worked at it.

There was nothing holding me to the bed which meant some more shuffling got my legs around to the edge and I was able to carefully sit up. In the dark, I was fearful I might encounter a low ceiling but found nothing but free air.

Okay, I was sitting up. Now what?

Still dredging my memory, I could not recall getting to my house. Everything went blank when I parked the car.

A sudden burst of light burned my eyes as the lights in the room came on. The walls, floor, and ceiling were all bright white and the lights set into the panels above my head were like those erected in a surgical theatre.

My eyes screwed tight shut to defend themselves, but even through my eyelids it still hurt.

'Ah, I see you are awake,' came a disembodied voice. Like the lights, the suddenness of it startled me, making me jolt. It was coming over a speaker, the voice containing that electronic not-quite-rightness and sounding distant even though it was right in the room.

I looked about but could not see the speaker. Guessing it was plastered into the wall, as they can be, I hopped to my feet and tried to find it.

'I hope you are feeling well,' the voice continued, 'and rested. Though not too rested because you will sleep again soon.'

I froze to the spot, my blood turning to ice because in that instant I knew who I was listening to. The Sandman had me. He threatened to sing me to sleep and now I was his captive.

A chuckle came over the airwaves. 'Did you just work it out, Jane Butterworth? Yes, I can see by your body language. There is no reason for alarm, Jane. Nothing terrible is going to happen to you. I merely wish to sing you to sleep. You probably expect me to harbour a grudge because you stole Karen Gilbert from me, yet I do not. I will find Karen again in time, and she can hear her song then.'

I looked around, trying not to appear frantic even though that was exactly how I felt.

Had I not been gagged I might have thought up a witty repartee or launched a salvo of expletives and threats. Since I could do neither, I focused on what I could do – I listened.

He sounded confident, that was the first thing that stuck in my head. His voice was that of a middle-aged man; someone the wrong side of fifty perhaps. His accent was local and educated, by which I mean he sounded like he had attended a private school and came from money. Kent has a gulf of divide between the multi-millionaires living in huge country houses and the breadline living-wage workers stuffed two families to a tiny house. The two live almost next door to each other in some areas.

There was also something familiar about his voice. My brain insisted I knew who I was listening to or that it was someone I had once met. If that were true, I could not yet connect a face to the voice.

The Sandman continued to prattle on, chatting away happily like we were sharing a conversation over a coffee. 'There is no point in looking for a way out, Jane. I'm afraid escape is quite impossible. You should rejoice though for all your worries are over. All the petty concerns you held for relationships, bills ... the future. All will melt away when I sing you to sleep for the final time.'

I hopped back to the bed but continued to look around the room until I spotted the camera lens. It was tiny - a fraction of an inch, no more. A small fraction at that. He could see me, he could hear me, and he held all the cards.

Well, maybe not quite all. My research led me to be convinced he had only ever killed women. According to everyone, my small frame makes me look scrawny when I am dressed as James. To be fair, I get what they are saying. I weigh not much more than a hundred pounds and I'm nearly six feet tall. However, when I choose to become Jane, the attributes change and suddenly I am thought to be willowy or slender – positives for a woman. Is it any wonder I spend more time as my feminine persona? Getting my voice to sound right took some time, but I was willing to bet the Sandman, whoever he was, had no idea about my true gender.

Grab your copy...
vinci-books.com/sandman

About the Author

When Steve Higgs wrote his debut novel, *Paranormal Nonsense*, he was a captain in the British Army. He would like to pretend that he had one of those careers that must be blacked out and generally denied by the government, and that he has to change his name and move constantly because he is still on the watch list in several countries. In truth, though, he started out as a mechanic - not like Jason Statham in the film by that name, sneaking around as a hitman, but more like one of those sleazy guys who charges a fortune and keeps your car for a week even though the only thing you went in for was a squeaky door hinge.

At school, he was largely disinterested in all subjects except creative writing, for which he won his first prize at the age of ten. However, calling it the first prize he won suggests that there were other prizes, which is not the case. Awards may yet come, but in the meantime, he enjoys writing mystery and thriller novels and claims to have more than a hundred books forming a restless queue in his mind because they are desperate to be written.

Now retired from the military, he lives in southeast England with a duo of lazy sausage dogs. Surrounded by rolling hills, brooding castles, and vineyards, he doubts he'll ever leave, the beer is just too good.

www.ingramcontent.com/pod-product-compliance
Ingram Content Group UK Ltd.
Pitfield, Milton Keynes, MK11 3LW, UK
UKHW041857120925
462873UK00004B/120

9 781036 708665